THE CURSE
OF THE
LION

THE CURSE
OF THE
LION

F. A. M. WEBSTER

COACHWHIP PUBLICATIONS

Greenville, Ohio

First published 1922.
Frederick Annesley Michael Webster (1886-1949)
No claims made on public domain material.

Front cover: Lion © Johan Swanepoel

CoachwhipBooks.com

ISBN 1-61646-282-5
ISBN-13 978-1-61646-282-6

CONTENTS

My Dear Tim,

When we both served in East Africa during the Great War, and after, when we roamed the bush and plains together in search of Game, these stories were often discussed, it maybe therefore that you will recognise some old friends both in fiction and fact and, I hope, much of the character of that land—Africa, which has cast its spell upon us, and many another beside, for all time.

She is an enduring old hag, grudging or over lavish of her favours, but we have learned to love her.

The bitter-sweet smell of the *maua* of the plains is still fresh in my nostrils and my eyes still hunger for the sight of the frangipani and the flaming hibiscus blossoms by Mombassa.

Shall I ever see it all again? I wonder!

Meanwhile, good hunting *"Toto ya Afric."*

These stories will be your Christmas present for 1922.

Kwa heri,

Michael.

Bromham, England.
August, 1922.

I
THE CURSE OF THE LION

I

IT WAS NEARLY MIDNIGHT. Three men were sitting in the study of a house in Regent Terrace, smoking, after a music-hall. One of them was sitting close to the fire, his bronzed aquiline features thrown into strong relief by the leaping flames. The two others shared a Chesterfield drawn somewhat back from the hearthrug and flanked by a Moorish coffee-stool, upon which stood a tray of glasses surrounding a decanter of whisky and a siphon of soda-water. Both men were in dress clothes, but Hugh Trent had already donned an old velvet smoking jacket belonging to his host.

"Those trick cyclists were good," said the other, Jack Spenser. "The hours those fellows must spend in training would put an Oxford athletic Blue to shame."

Hugh nodded as he leant forward and applied a light to his cigar.

"Didn't think much of those black magicians," Jack continued. "People always rave about the mysterious powers of the coloured races, but, personally, I think their alleged supernatural gifts are mostly sleight of hand or hypnotism."

At that moment a lion roared loud and long from the Zoological Gardens across the Park.

"Do either of you fellows remember Tom Harden?" asked Bruce Logan from his seat by the fireside.

"Yes," answered Hugh, removing his cigar. "He was a member of the Sports Club. You remember him, Jack, surely. That great,

9

deep-chested fellow who always sat in the far corner of the smoking-room, with a big meerschaum pipe between his teeth. He never mixed much with people, but I should have thought you would have known him. One used to see him in the Club every day for a month or two, and then he would disappear into the wilds of Africa or some other God-forsaken place for two or three years."

"Oh, I remember him well enough," said Jack; "big-game hunter, wasn't he?"

"Yes," said Bruce; "he took me with him on one of his hunting trips, about the end of 1902. I'd been knocking about Egypt for a few months and met him in Old Bourse Street on my return to Alexandria. We dined together at the Victoria Club and went on to the 'Mahomet Ali' afterwards. I remember that I had made up my mind to go down to Port Said for a few days before catching a boat for Marseilles. Over coffee he started talking about big-game, and somehow his description of the East African wilds fired my imagination. There was no real reason why I should come home, and the end of it all was that I bought some new guns next day, and a week later found myself on board a boat steaming down the Red Sea, bound for Mombassa. Africa was all, and more than all, that he'd promised me. The heat waves beat into our faces as we passed Mombassa and steamed into Kilindini harbour. The scent of the frangi-pani was well-nigh overpowering, and the blaze of the flaming hibiscus blossoms bordering the white ribbon of road almost blinded our eyes when we stepped ashore.

"Africa seemed to have laid a spell upon Tom, for he was like a man newly returned to his home after a long absence. He spoke Arabic and the Swahili language like a native, and one could see at a glance that the natives not only knew, but liked him. In these circumstances we had no difficulty in getting hold of good cooks, personal boys, and gun-bearers. From Mombassa we went up by the Uganda Railway to Nairobi, where we fitted out a *safari*—that is to say, a hunting expedition—and trekked out into the wilds at the head of a column of a hundred caravan porters carrying our loads.

"We had been trekking for a month before we got to the locality for which we were making. It was a perfectly wild and practically unexplored part. Tom told me he had never been there before. He had heard long since that the country literally teemed with big-game—and there was quite a decent chance of bagging an okapi. It is as you may know, an extremely rare beast. No specimen had been obtained up to that time and the chance of getting one was the prime cause of our journey north, but the more nearly we approached our destination the more persistent became the rumours concerning a strange race said to inhabit the unknown territory. So far as we could gather from the wild natives whom Tom questioned, these people were neither of Bantu nor Nilotic stock; they were a race apart, called by the natives 'The Strange People.'

"I shall never forget my first sight of them.

"Early one morning we were smoking our after-breakfast pipes and watching Mnyogi, our head-man, allotting the burdens for the day's march, when Tom suddenly jumped up and pointed to the brow of the hill some fifty yards away. I looked in the direction he indicated, and saw a huge savage who must have been quite six and a half feet in height. His features were thin and, to use an objectionable word, 'aristocratic.' Upon his head was a great plume of feathers; from his shoulders depended a magnificent leopard skin; at his right thigh swung a cross-hilted sword, and in his left hand he held a buffalo-hide shield which completely covered his body from shoulder to mid-thigh; from behind it there protruded the points of three or four formidable spears. The amazing thing about the man was his colour, for he was little darker than a great many Italians I have known. As we rose from our camp chairs he threw up his right hand in greeting or menace—we had no means of telling which—before he disappeared behind the hill. This evidence of the truth of the native rumours greatly excited Tom.

"We marched steadily on through the heat of the day; towards evening we came upon a great cluster of grass huts set about a hill. That something unusual was taking place was evident, for all the inhabitants of the village seemed to be assembled around a tall tree upon the top of the hill. As we drew nearer we saw a figure, which we took to be that of a baboon or big monkey, perched amongst the topmost branches. On closer inspection this proved to be a man of great age. How he managed to maintain himself in that insecure position was a mystery. No notice was taken as we marched through the village and climbed the hill. We halted at the edge of the circle of natives about the tree, from the top of which the old man was speaking in a sort of bastard Arabic, which we followed with some little difficulty. So far as we could make out, he was enumerating the places within three days' journey of the village at which elephants had died recently. He brought his oration to an end with the amazing statement that from his tree-top he had actually *seen* the elephants die. We learned subsequently that he seldom left his eerie, I do not know, therefore how else he could have obtained the news. He may have watched the flight of the vultures, but in that case he would only have known there was a dead body about, he could not have said it was that of an elephant—and yet his information never proved incorrect. When the séance—I can call it nothing else—was over, certain armed parties set off across the surrounding plains in various directions. The old man then descended from his perch and gravely shook us by the hand, according to the Soudanese fashion in which, after the palms have met, the thumb is grasped and the performance repeated. He then inquired the reason of our journey and offered us the hospitality of his village, after which he again ascended the tree trunk to his perch, nearly eighty feet above the ground.

Luckily we had plenty of tinned stuff with us and the hind quarters of a buck I had shot in the forenoon, for we found that these people followed the Masai custom of living on bullock's blood mixed with milk. They never ate solid food. After we had been in the village a few days and had begun to find the hunting excellent, Mnyogi came to our tent early one morning.

"'Masters,' said he, 'these drinkers of blood worship a lion.'

"'What do you say?' asked Tom. 'And where is this lion who is their god?'

"'He lives near here,' answered the gun-bearer, 'for have we not heard him roaring at night? Moreover, to him they sacrifice not only cattle, but women and children also at certain seasons. Of late he has refused the cattle, asking always for human flesh.'

"'How do you know all this, Mnyogi?' asked Tom.

"'The maidens speak of it, master,' he replied.

"'And what have you to do with the maidens?' Tom queried.

"For a moment Mnyogi stood debating his answer, then: 'There is one that I would buy, Bwana, but she is to be given to the lion at the next festival.'

"Tom's face lit up with pleasurable anticipation.

"'What do you say to some lion hunting soon, Bruce?' he said in English, for he did not wish Mnyogi to know what was in his mind.

"We made cautious inquiry as to the possibility of killing lion in the neighbouring bush, but met always with evasive answers, some of the tribesmen even going to the length of denying that they had ever seen a lion. This was manifestly absurd, for each evening between sunset and nine o'clock—the lions' hunting hours—we heard the great brutes grunting and calling to each other.

"Now the peculiar coughing grunt with which a lion announces his intention of hunting is a very different matter to the full-bodied roar which he uses sometimes to celebrate his kill and sometimes just for the sake of hearing his own voice. At that time I had never heard a lion roar, although I had been in Africa six months.

"During the three days following upon our gun-bearer's announcement we continued to collect trophies and to hunt for the okapi, as we had done for a week past, but we kept a sharp look out for lion's spoor. That we never came across any tracks is probably due to the fact that the chief had lent us several of his own hunters to act as guides—and they, no doubt, took good care to keep us away from the haunts of their tribal deity.

"On the fourth day a band of warriors came in followed by a long column of women carrying upon their heads magnificent ivory tusks taken from elephants that had died some twenty-four hours' march away and which the old wizard chief had 'seen' from the top of his tree.

"Certain of these tusks were selected and taken to the 'Chief's Pallisade.' This was, in reality, a wonderful fence of crossed elephants' tusks surrounding the ground in which the wizard would some day be buried. It was said that the old man had 'seen' elephants and ruled the tribe for a hundred years and for just that time the fence had been building.

"That night we kept to our tent, for a great *ngoma* was taking place. When the dance reached its climax a bull was slaughtered and the savages began drinking the reeking blood raw and unqualified by boiling milk as was their usual custom. I didn't like the look of things at all as I peered out through the tent opening; I said as much to Tom, who was sitting on his camp bed filling a pipe. Before he could reply a lion roared once and instantly the pandemonium of the dance ceased. It was the most extraordinary sight. Men and women stood still as if paralysed by a sudden, awful command. The blood of the slaughtered bull soaked unheeded into the sand, the drums fell silent and even the eyes of the dancers remained set in an awful, vacant stare.

"I felt the hair rising upon my scalp and then the tension was broken. Evidently the lion had crept up closer, until he was only just beyond the circle of the firelight.

"Suddenly he roared again and yet again; instantly every native— warrior or woman—dropped flat and lay rigid with outstretched hands.

"The noise the lions make at the Zoo at feeding time is foolery compared with the row that chap kicked up. He just roared and roared to emphasise his majesty. It was the most awful sound, or series of sounds, I have ever heard. The very substance of the earth seemed to shake, the air trembled. The repeated volleys rumbled into silence, and it seemed as if all the Wild—human and animal— was crouched in rigid terror beneath the menace of that mighty voice.

"There must have been something hypnotic in the performance, for I came to myself with a start when Tom, with his rifle grasped in his right hand, dropped his left upon my shoulder and shoved me quietly away from the opening. In a minute I had gripped him by the arm and swung him back into the tent, for I had seen the effect of the lion's roaring upon the savages and knew what their temper would be like if they saw Tom appear, rifle in hand and prepared to deal with their pet fetish.

"Next morning before it was light Mnyogi burst into the tent and shook Tom roughly by the shoulder, a most improper and un-precedented performance, promptly punished by a straight left which landed the gun-bearer half out of the doorway by which he had entered.

"When the man had regained his feet Tom cut short his mumb-led apologies and asked him what was the matter. Immediately it appeared that the lion had called to be fed last night and that Menharria, the lady of our gun-bearer's affections, was missing this morning. The inference was obvious.

"It may be said that Tom was foolishly quixotic or that he re-pented handling the native so roughly. We were both genuinely fond of the boy, who had proved himself a brave and faithful ser-vant on more than one occasion.

"'I'm going after that lion,' said Tom. 'I don't think he's healthy to have about the place, he might take to fancying white flesh next.'

"Mnyogi crept out. In a few minutes he returned with my gun-bearer, an undersized Nandi, called Kibrono, as ugly as sin, but absolutely to be depended upon in a tight place.

"Mnyogi unlaced the back flap of the tent and stole ahead of us into the gathering light. We passed through the village as silently as ghosts, leaving by a way we had never taken before. Mnyogi, however, seemed to know where he was going. No sooner were we in the bush than we struck a narrow track up which we had to crawl bent double, for it was no more than four and a half feet high. We were compelled to follow our hunter in single file. After about twenty minutes of slow progress through this prickly tunnel, we emerged into an open space enclosed in the heart of the forest. Across the clearing the half obscured opening of a cave showed dimly, all around it lay a litter of bones, picked clean by the hyenas and bleached white by the sun. There were skulls of buck and bullock and there were skulls of sheep, but the remains which fixed our attention were those of human beings.

"Suddenly a ray of sunlight shot down through the branches of the trees. It struck full into the mouth of the cave where lay the bloody, mangled remains of Menharria. Mnyogi gave a short, gasping cry and made to spring forward, but I gripped him by the arm. At the same moment a lion, which we had not up to then perceived, rose up and slid off an ant heap where he had been sleeping. The beast uttered one low, rumbling growl of warning. Mnyogi struggled wildly to break away from my grip, and thus prevented me from using my rifle. Tom bade Mnyogi sharply to be quiet. At the same moment he raised his rifle. Just as he pressed the trigger the lion charged. The bullet took him in the neck and stopped him for a fraction of a second, just long enough, in fact, for Tom to reload. That lion looked enormous and came at the speed of an express train. I let Mnyogi go and flung up my rifle, but as I did so Tom fired again, a beautiful shot fair between the eyes. The lion turned tail upwards and began to thrash around tearing up the earth in great lumps.

"Before the beast was dead we saw the Wizard of the Tree standing in the mouth of the cave. How he got there one cannot imagine, but there he was, his fierce eyes blazing, the thin white hair of his head fairly bristling and his emaciated frame trembling with rage.

"'You have killed my Lord the Lion!' he shrieked, pointing a trembling finger at Tom. 'You have killed my Lord the Lion! The curse of the Lion be upon you! Whither you go he shall follow and when he calls you shall answer his calling. Go! you have been the guest of my people. Go! and the curse of the Lion go with you! We may not kill our guest, but my Lord the Lion shall claim his own again. I have spoken!'"

* * * * * *

Bruce got up from the arm-chair and helped himself to a whisky and soda.

"Pretty uncanny ending to our hunting expedition, wasn't it? And we didn't get an okapi either."

He sat down again by the fire and began to scrape out the bowl of his pipe.

II

"It's deuced late," said Jack, looking at his watch. "Can I give you a lift, Hugh? I ought to have gone earlier, but I thought Bruce was going to tell us something unusual about the alleged magic of the black man."

Hugh did not move from the corner of the Chesterfield.

"Wasn't Harden killed in rather peculiar circumstances a few years ago, Bruce?" he asked.

"Yes," said Bruce, "I was going to tell you about it."

Jack on his way to the door paused and turned half round. He looked across at Bruce with a puzzled expression.

"Had his death anything to do with lions?" he queried.

"Wait and listen," said Hugh. "We'll get a taxi all right later on."

Jack turned back to the fire. Picked up a cigarette from a side table and lit it.

"Go on, Bruce," he said.

Bruce deliberately finished scraping out his pipe and filled it. Then he lay back in his arm-chair, puffing thoughtfully. For a few moments there was silence in the room.

"I didn't see much of Tom after we got back to England. He spent his usual month at the Club reading, smoking and studying maps; then I heard that he'd gone to China, or the South Seas, no one quite knew which. I must confess that I felt pretty badly hurt that he should have gone off again without a word of farewell to me, after all we had been through together.

"Soon after his departure I became engaged and so dropped out of the way of frequenting the Club. Consequently I lost touch with most of the men who might have given me news of him.

"After eighteen months my engagement was broken off, but I had already taken this place, in view of my approaching marriage, so I came here to live. I expected at first to be pretty badly bothered by the beasts at the Zoo, but it is surprising how little noise they make. That lion's roar we heard to-night is the first sound I have heard from the Gardens for a long time. Towards the end of the second year after I moved here, I met a man at a luncheon party one day who told me he had seen Bruce in Cairo a few weeks previously and that he was looking worried and ill. I came home late one night and my man met me in the hall. He told me that a gentlemen was in the study and had been waiting for me for nearly three hours. Wilkins said that he thought the gentleman was ill because the last time he had gone in to make up the fire he had found him asleep.

"I walked across the hall and opened the study door and here in this very arm-chair I saw poor old Tom sound asleep. I stood still for a moment or two studying him. There was still the same lofty, intolerant look that I knew so well but he looked a trifle fine-drawn and his features seemed sharper than I remembered them. His skin was tanned almost black and yet there was a curious grey tinge beneath the flesh, under his eyes were deep circles, and a fine network of wrinkles spread fan-wise from the corners of the lids.

"Just as I was about to speak the long-drawn, whining call of a hyena echoed across the Park. Tom awoke instantly. I was surprised to recognise the outline of a heavy revolver which weighed down the right hand pocket of his jacket, for it had not been his custom to carry firearms, except when actually in the wilds.

"'What was that?' he gasped, starting up and I noticed that his voice shook on a tense note of fear.

"I hastened across the room to reassure him.

"'It was only an old *fisi* in the Zoo across the Park,' I laughed.

"As my hand fell upon his shoulder I was horrified to find that no more than a mere bag of bones was concealed beneath the clothing.

"'Good God, Tom!' I exclaimed. 'Why, man, you're only skin and bone; where's all the muscle and flesh gone to?'

"He laughed in an embarrassed sort of way and his greeting was almost feverish.

"'Where are you staying?' I asked, intending to give him a chance to pull himself together a bit; I was therefore somewhat surprised by his answer.

"'I haven't fixed anything up yet,' he said; 'I only landed this morning. I went straight to the Club for dinner when I reached London. De Courville gave me your address. I came round because I cannot sleep until we've had a talk.'

"I rang for Wilkins and told him to prepare a room at once. I was determined not to let Tom out of my sight again until I knew what was troubling him.

"After some supper we settled down in here. Wilkins put the whisky and soda ready on the little table between us and asked if he might go to bed.

"When he had gone and our pipes were in full blast Tom looked across at me.

"'Do you believe that curses ever work?' he asked.

"'It depends a good deal on what you mean by curses,' I answered guardedly.

"'I'm cursed,' he said wearily.

"I said nothing, but waited for him to tell me more if he felt inclined. The reading lamp on the desk was shaded, but the glow of the fire lit up his face dimly and I could see that he was struggling for words with which to explain his meaning.

"'I've been cursed ever since we left Tirkanaland,' he continued, at last. 'That old Tree Wizard cursed me after I'd shot the lion and, my God, he had the power to do it.'

"I smiled.

"'You probably wondered why I went off abroad again without seeing you,' he continued. 'It was because I was ashamed to tell you that I was beginning to be afraid. You remember how we were bothered by lions all the way down country until we reached Nairobi; but you did not know, because I did not tell you, that every time I heard a lion roar I felt an almost irresistible desire to go out to him.'

"'Once I got back to England I swore that I'd never set foot in a lion country again, but the lure of Africa was in my blood and before I'd been home a month I found myself longing to be back again amongst the Somalis and the Masai. For a time the thought of lions ceased to bother me, but all the same I dared not go back to Africa and yet I wanted to, aye, longed to. I was soul-hungry for the smell of the dust on the plains and the sweltering, sweating heat in the bush. I knew that if I waited another week I'd just give in and go, so I booked a passage to China to see what the sight of new lands and strange peoples would do for me.

"'Bruce! I tell you it was no good,' he said. 'I tried China, Japan and the South Seas. I went down to the Solomon Islands and came away rotten with yaws. I tried the Malay Archipelago and nearly got my throat slit for my pains. Then I had a go at bear in the Rockies. Man! I've lived in a whirl of adventure these last two years and more incidents have piled themselves one on top of the other, than I could ever tell you of.'

"I nodded with sympathy.

"'It hasn't been the slightest use,' he continued. 'I might just as well have stopped in the Sports Club reading and hearing about other fellows' travels. In the midst of each adventure and at the climax of each new excitement a quiet voice has seemed to call me to come back to Africa. The mystery and charm of that land are over me and I'd give my soul to go back to it all and yet I daren't—because an old Tree Wizard put the Curse of the Lion upon me. I know that if I go back to the lion country one of the brutes will get me sooner or later. Yet I'm not afraid of death, for I've faced death in a hundred forms every month of these last two years. Curious, isn't it?'

"I looked at him for a long moment, and then I asked him a question.

"'What makes you think that a lion will get you, Tom?' I said.

"'Because every night of my life I dream that lions are after me,' he answered, 'and always the dream ends in the same way. One particular brute with a great black mane singles me out; he never springs, but rears up above me and, just as his huge paw is sweeping down to strike, I awaken.'

"'Is there nothing more than this dream that worries you?' I asked.

"'Yes,' he replied. 'I cannot bear to hear a lion roar nor to listen to the long-drawn-out whine of the hyena, his parasite. You saw how I started up when that *fisi* called to-night?'

"In vain I argued, entreated and pointed out the utter folly of the delusions from which he was suffering—at least I thought they were delusions then. He quite agreed with me that an overwrought imagination might play strange tricks, and he was perfectly willing to go into a sanatorium for a complete rest cure if I thought it would do him good. But nothing could shake his belief that sooner or later the call of Africa would prove too strong for him and, equally, he was sure that if he did go to Africa he would fall a victim to lions, a big one with a black mane, to be particular.

"It was not long past midnight when we went to bed and I was glad to see that Wilkins had had the good sense to light a fire in Tom's room, for the snow lay deep on the ground outside and his blood was thinned by long sojourning in the Tropics.

"The moment I was in bed I fell into a heavy sleep, for I was very tired. After what seemed a long time I half awakened from a dream in which I had seemed to hear a lion roaring close at hand and the patter of bare feet along the passage. I turned over and went to sleep again, certain that the dream had been induced by the recital of poor Tom's afflictions.

"A few minutes before three o'clock I woke up again. This time there was no question of dreams. There was not one beast roaring but a full dozen. It was a noise such as a pride of lions make when they have deliberately driven game into a closed ravine where the killers are waiting and they wish to celebrate the slaughter.

"Hastily throwing on a dressing gown I ran along the passage to Tom's room, thinking that the fearful racket would pretty well frighten him to death in his present nervous condition. When I reached the door it was wide open! I switched on the electric light and saw that the room was empty. My hand placed between the cold sheets told me that Tom must have been gone some time. I ran quickly downstairs and switched on the hall light. My study door was open and I could feel the bitter night air blowing in through the open window.

"I slipped into a pair of gum boots, and put a thick coat on over my dressing gown, snatched up my electric torch from the hall stand and went back into the study.

"I leant out of the window. By the aid of the concentrated beam from my torch I could easily distinguish the imprints of bare feet in the deep white snow. I lowered myself to the ground prepared to take up the trail. At that moment a policeman came in sight. I explained the position and my strange attire by saying that a friend of mine, recently returned from the East, had left the house, either walking in his sleep or in a state of delirium.

"Together we followed the easily-read spoor, and all the time those infernal lions kept up their unholy racket. I remember the policeman remarking that he had never before heard them behave so strangely in all the time he had been in the district.

"The footprints led us straight to the fencing that encloses the Zoological Gardens. I pulled myself up to the top and could see by the aid of my torch the trail still leading away upon the other side.

"At this point the policeman wished to find a keeper to open a gate, but I told him I was going on whether he came or not and that if he wanted to stop me he would have to use force and a pair of handcuffs. He was a good fellow and came readily enough after a little persuasion.

"The spoor was so plain in the untrodden snow within the en-closure that we were able to follow it at a run. As we approached the lions' house the roaring rose to a final crescendo of triumph. Suddenly it gave place to absolute silence.

"The terrific din had evidently awakened others besides my-self. As we reached the door two keepers hurried up.

"A few brief words explained both my presence and my fears. A second later the door swung open and we entered.

"Something dimly white gleamed in front of one of the centre cages. As our eyes focused upon the barely visible form the second keeper snapped on the electric light.

"Poor Tom, in his night-clothes, was stretched face downwards between the protection rail and the front bars of the cage. His head had been smashed in by one terrific blow; behind the bars a great, black-maned lion lay licking his paw. Around the claws blood and hair were clotted."

* * * * * *

Bruce leaned forward and knocked the ashes from his pipe. All three men were silent, thinking each in his own fashion of the mysterious powers which lie concealed in the unfathomable minds of the native races whose psychology and customs we do not, nor ever shall, understand.

Bruce got up and walked over to the window. He drew the curtain aside and looked into the night. Outside snow was falling fast. Suddenly a clock in the hall clanged out two deep notes. Hugh started to his feet and crossed to the door.

"Good-night, Bruce!" he said, softly.

He picked up his hat and coat. Jack followed him silently from the room.

II
A KILLING PALAVER

WILKINS HAD FINISHED removing the remains of his master's dinner and stood attentively waiting while Bruce Logan prepared his own brew of Turkish coffee in a specially devised machine which stood upon the sideboard. The fragrance of the beverage filled all the dark, oak-panelled room of the big house in Regent Terrace. A moment later the bubbling liquid was transferred from the glass retort to a thin Limogés cup. Wilkins, coming forward, took it up and carried it over to the Moorish stool set beside Logan's deep chair, drawn close to the fire of blazing logs.

"Will you require anything else, sir?"

"Nothing."

As the door closed softly behind the servant, Logan sank into the chair and stretched his long legs towards the cheery blaze. He rubbed his strong, sun-burned hands together ruminatively, for he was tasting the bitter-sweet memories of the outland places, where so many years of his life had been spent and seeing again the wind-swept, sun-washed plains where the buck and zebra roam in herds of a thousand head.

Presently his attention was attracted by the clang of the front door bell. After a while, Wilkins entered to announce Hugh Trent and Jack Spenser.

"Come along in," said Logan. "I was praying that someone would look me up for a yarn. The 'black butterflies' have me this evening and I'm longing for the waste places of the world."

"The old wander-lust, eh?" smiled Trent.

Jack Spenser cast himself down upon the Chesterfield and looked expectantly towards Wilkins.

"Whisky or brandy, sir?" queried the servant.

"Whisky, please, and just the least dash of soda."

Trent produced a pipe and felt in his pocket for his pouch.

"Plenty of tobacco in the rhino's foot upon the sideboard," murmured Logan; then added: "I don't suppose you will try this?"; he reached up his hand to the mantelpiece for a strangely-carved Indian *yogi* jug containing pungent Boer tobacco and slowly filled an enormous meerschaum pipe.

For a while the three friends smoked in silence. At last Spenser spoke.

"That was a queer yarn you told us the other evening about the 'Curse of the Lion,' which was placed upon poor Tom Harden."

"Strange, indeed," agreed Logan; "but I've met other things as strange in my wanderings. I tell you," he continued firmly and emphasising each word, "the natives of Africa hold powers which are entirely beyond our understanding."

"What sort of powers?" asked Trent, with the obvious intention of drawing a story from his host.

"What sort of powers, do you ask? Devilish powers! So awful in their workings as to make your blood run cold; to make you ask if there is a God to allow such atrocities.

"The worst case I ever came across was at Kema, an island five degrees south of the Equator and midway between Mombassa and Dar-es-Salaam.

"After Harden's uncanny death in the Lions' House at the Zoological Gardens the desire came upon me to go back to Africa and to square accounts with the Tree Wizard of the Strange People, who had laid the Curse of the Lion upon my friend. Of my return to the land of the Strange People, where the elephants' graveyard is, I will tell you some other time. For the moment I need only tell you that I got into the country with an ivory seeker sent up by the Sudan Government. After our affair was over, I made my way down country to Nairobi where I stayed several months shaking off a bad attack of dysentery.

"By the time I was well again the spell of Africa had claimed me, the love of the land was in my blood and the scent of Africa bemused my brain.

"From Nairobi I drifted down to Mombassa, and from that place made my way to Zanzibar, where I managed to get a Government job. My first home leave was due in August, 1914, but all leave was cancelled upon the outbreak of war, nor could any of us get permission to go to England to join the new armies. Perhaps I was luckier than the rest, or perhaps I had more influence—at any rate, I got permission to join the Zanzibar battalion of the King's African Rifles, which was, at that time, raised for war service.

"We messed about on the parade ground, forming fours, presenting arms and skirmishing for weeks on end, and then I was detailed to go to Kema to recruit native labour for the Military Labour Corps. It was not the sort of service to which I had been looking forward, but nothing could be worse than the interminable squad drill upon the barrack square; and, moreover, I was anxious to see this island of sinister repute, which I had not previously visited during my three years' sojourn in Africa.

"There were strange tales told of the island of Kema, tales of devil worship and human sacrifice, crimes the Government could never prove and the existence of which was, therefore, denied. The natives of Zanzibar knew a great deal more of these matters than they cared to say; indeed, it was impossible to get either the educated Arabs or the coastwise Swahilis to talk about Kema at all.

"The day before my detachment was due to embark I broached the subject to my old platoon sergeant, a Nubian named Musa bin Mahommed, asking him what strange things we might expect to find on this *safari*, as we call an expedition.

"'Who can say, Effendi?' he replied. 'Allah knows all, but there are many things of which the Faithful may not speak, and the *washenzi** of the island have strange customs.'

"On the night of our arrival upon Kema, Musa came to my tent after *tamam* parade, or, as you would say, 'Roll Call.'

"'Effendi,' he said, 'a *shenzi** has been in the lines asking the *asikari*† whither we journey and why. I would have brought him to you, but at my approach he made off at a great pace into the bush.'

"At the time I thought little of the matter, judging the inquiry to be prompted by the inexhaustible curiosity of the African native.

"Next morning we moved out of bivouac, fifty fighting men and a hundred *wapagazi* (that is 'caravan porters') to carry the loads. The little column moved along the forest paths in the peculiar formation always adopted by the K.A.R. when marching through country in which hostilities may eventuate at any moment. The damp heat was terrific, and all the while I felt that eyes were marking our progress from the dense bush which fills in the interstices between the tree trunks; these, incidentally, are covered with a peculiarly repulsive grey parasitic growth. Day after day we pushed on in the humid heat; my limbs were in a continuous bath of sweat and each night when we made camp the malaria-carrying mosquitoes made life unbearable.

"On the fifth afternoon we halted and made our *boma*‡ not far from a fair-sized village. That night I filled myself up with quinine and aspirin and went to bed early, for I was rotten with malaria. Next day I spent recruiting labour in the village, but I was determined to push forward at dawn the following morning.

"In the middle of the night I was awakened by Musa.

"'Effendi, come quickly!' he said; 'for there is a killing *shauri*¶ and the *wapagazi* are gone.'

"Hastily pulling on my mosquito boots, into which I tucked the legs of my trousers, I snatched up my revolver and followed Musa to the corner of the *boma* allotted to the *wapagazi*. Sure enough

---

* *Shenzi* is a term of contempt, meaning "wild native."

† Soldiers.

‡ Camp within a strong thorn fence.

¶ Business or affair.

they were gone and all their personal belongings with them. The manner of their departure was quite plain, too, for the thorn fence was torn down and cast aside, leaving a twelve-foot opening.

"'Come, Effendi,' said Musa, and held up his lantern to light my way through the torn and crampled thorn scrub.

"Immediately we were beyond the fence my eye was caught by the gleam of another lantern around which dim shapes moved restlessly. We drew nearer and I saw a huddled 'something' stretched upon the ground in the midst of the group. It was the khaki-clad, bare-armed body of the sentry whose duty it was to patrol the side of the *boma* where the *wapagazi* slept. In vain we searched his body for marks of violence. At last Musa's thin hands questing over the smooth, brown flesh were arrested by contact with a small hard lump at the base of the dead man's neck.

"With a muttered exclamation he rose upright and I saw upon the palm of his extended hand a tiny poisoned dart such as the bush folk use. It was plain then that the sentry had been struck down by someone outside the *boma* from which the porters, seeing him fall, had, for their own reasons, departed. We rebuilt the fence as best we could and doubled the sentries.

"With the first streak of dawn showing in the sky I paraded the detachment and marched into the village where I proposed to hold stringent inquiry into the murder. I assembled the chief and his councilors and made it quite plain to them that this was a hanging palaver in which many would suffer if the murderers were not caught and brought to justice within four and twenty hours.

"I left the village well garrisoned and Sergeant Musa bin Mahommed in charge and went back to my tent in the *boma* to think matters over. One thing, at all events, was abundantly clear, that without *wapagazi* to carry the loads I could not hope to push forward any further, nor could I commandeer fresh porters from the village, for the labour I had recruited but yesterday was now well on its way down to the coast.

"There was no moon at that season. When dark had fallen and a man might move about unobserved, a dark shape came wriggling on its stomach to the edge of the ring of light thrown by my lantern.

I slipped my revolver from its holster and let the muzzle dwell upon the figure of my unexpected visitor.

"'Whence come you, man, and why?' I asked.

"'*Bwana*,' whispered a voice out of the shadows, 'I come to tell you true things, that the people of my village may not suffer.'

"'Speak on,' I answered.

"'*Bwana*,' he said again, 'I have served the Government in irons and have suffered for my sins, but am now a true man, knowing and fearing the might of the *Serkali*.'*

"'It may be with reason that you know and fear; speak on,' I replied."

Logan paused and took a long drink from the tall tumbler at his side. He got up and wandered about the big room for a few minutes. Presently he reached up to a shield of trophies hanging upon the wall, from which he selected a curiously curved knife. Returning to his seat by the fireside he fingered the weapon meditatively for a moment before placing it upon the Moorish coffee stool beside him. After thinking for the space occupied in refilling his big meerschaum pipe, he continued his story.

"Meanwhile," he said, "strange things had happened, according to the statement of my visitor the ex-convict, at the principal town in the interior at which I had hoped to recruit the major portion of the labour required.

"The native who had visited our lines upon the day of landing had, apparently, gleaned some information which he had passed swiftly, by means known only to the natives themselves, to his chief at the inland town.

"That hoary-headed old ruffian thereupon had set the *ngomas** beating to assemble his people and had led them to a clearing in the heart of the forest. Then when the great fires were kindled they had squatted in a wide circle waiting for their overlord to speak. But he, too, was waiting.

---

* Government.
* Native drums made of skins stretched tight over hollow tree-trunks.

"Presently the medicine men appeared, painted variously and strung about with bones, snake-skins and little bladders.

"'My children,' said the old man, 'the *wachawi* (the wizards) are here, for the white man is upon his way with soldiers to carry our sons away to bear burdens for the *Serkali*; shall our young men go forth at his bidding?'

"'They shall not go,' answered the people.

"'How shall we save them?' asked the chief.

"'The *wachawi* shall save them,' answered the people.

"'Speak, oh Wizards,' cried the chief, 'how shall our children be saved from the white men?'

"Now the witch doctors danced and leapt, darting hither and thither so that the flames of firelight were flung back from their paint-smeared bodies; the necklaces of bones rattled and their hair, in which the little bladders were intertwined, streamed out behind them as they ran. Save for the rattling of the bones, the quick patter of bare feet and the deep breathing of the people no sound broke the silence of the forest.

"Suddenly the chief witch-doctor flung up his hand and shouted. Instantly all his companions became rigid as rods, while a little gasp of anticipation broke from the eager, waiting multitude.

"'Ha!' coughed the doctor. 'The white man comes, but we shall stop him. Ha! The white man comes, but he shall see nothing. Ha! The white man seeks, but he shall not find anything.'

"Again they danced and again stopped.

"'Ha,' he cried again. 'The white man is six days on his journey, bring therefore a six days' child.'

"Presently a week-old baby was brought and laid on the ground at his feet.

"'With thy sight passes the power of the white man to see our people, unless he find new eyes,' muttered the fiend. There was a long-drawn piercing wail.

"The horrible business continued until the wretched child was blind, deaf and dumb, that I might neither see the road to their village, hear any word of their doings, nor speak of anything I might learn. Finally they buried the little one alive that, with his death, the 'life of my journeying' might also pass.

"Observe that the sacrifice was consummated between midnight and dawn of the fifth and sixth days of our march, and that on the fifth night, when I was down with fever, the sentry over the *boma* was killed, and the porters, who were in fact, 'the life of my journeying,' deserted in a body.

"As the man at the edge of the lamp-light finished telling me this gruesome story, I flung myself forward out of my chair and pinned him to the ground.

"'How do you know these things?' I asked.

"'*Bwana*, I know,' he said, 'for I was hunting in the forest. When I saw the fires spring up at the forbidden place of sacrifice I drew near and watched. Then, knowing well what would happen if the people of the town discovered me, I crept softly away and ran swiftly back to my own village. I reached here this afternoon and heard of your words to us, spoken this morning.'

"I thought for a moment, still holding him down.

"'You know the place,' I said, 'therefore you shall be my "new eyes" of which the Mchawi spoke.'

"I felt his body tremble and shrink under my hand. Next moment he well-nigh overwhelmed me with a voluble outburst of protest against my proposition. But I was firm and once he realised that he would be one of those I should require in payment for last night's murder if he refused to guide me, he was quick enough to fall in with my wishes.

"For a white man it was three days' full journey to the place where the prohibited custom had been revived. I have told you, I was without porters, none the less I was now determined to get there at all costs.

"Next morning I sent our runners in every direction to find mules, but it was three days before they returned, and then they brought but half a dozen of the beasts. The best of these I took myself and upon the remaining five loaded such baggage as was absolutely indispensable. Musa I left in charge of the village with thirty *asikari* to act as garrison, the remaining twenty soldiers I paraded early in the morning of the day following the mules' arrival, and with them marched into the forest on the way to the big town. My ex-convict, whose name was Machunga, marched with his wrists strapped behind him and attached by a rope to my belt. I was none too sure that he had not invented his amazing yarn for the purpose of dividing my small force and getting me away from his own village.

"On the fourth morning we reached our destination as the first rosy flush of dawn was stealing up the sky.

"Looking down the steep hillside from the edge of the bush I saw a cluster of huts stretching up and down the banks of a small river, swollen to a torrent by the rains which had fallen during the past three days.

"No one was stirring as yet. Only the native chickens wandered and scratched among the apparently deserted dwellings.

"A whispered word of command sent my twenty *asikari* stealing down the hillside to surround the village.

"Allowing them a quarter of an hour to take up their positions I walked into the place and up to the door of the largest hut, crying '*Hodi!*'—which means 'Is any one in?' There was a stir of agitated movement inside but no answering cry of '*Karibu!*' which means 'Come near,' and is equivalent to an invitation to enter. I waited a moment longer, then pulled aside the mat which hung before the door and entered.

"An old man lay upon a bed and a couple of badly scared women crouched upon the ground in the corner.

"'Where is the chief?' I asked.

"Before the old man could reply one of the two women set up a terrified howling and I heard people rushing out of the huts all around me. In every direction they ran, but everywhere they were turned back and herded together by the levelled rifles of my well-posted sentries.

"I grabbed the old man by the shoulder and heaved him out into the sunlight. He chattered excitedly like a monkey, but did not attempt to escape.

"'Now,' I said, 'tell me where is your chief?'

"'*Bwana*,' said he, 'the chief and all the fighting men went out a month since to hunt in the forest and have not yet returned.'

"That I knew to be a lie, if the story told to me by Machunga the ex-convict could be relied upon.

"'Where then are your witch-doctors?' I asked next.

"'*Bwana!*' he answered in scandalised tones, 'We have no witch-doctors, for is not the practice of witchcraft forbidden by the *Serkali?* We be law-abiding folk whose ways are open as the sun at noon for all men to see.'

"'You did not, for example, hold a killing palaver at the rising of the moon?' I suggested.

"'Bwana,' he replied, 'an evil spirit has undoubtedly put such thoughts into your head.'

"That night when it was quite dark I collected the women, about fifty of them, their children and the half dozen old men who had been left behind in the village. These I sent back to Musa under escort of a corporal and four *asikari*.

"That left me with a force of but fifteen all told to deal with whatever trouble might eventuate. This little force I kept well concealed in the huts and the surrounding bush during the day-time. After waiting forty-eight hours we made our first capture. A scout passed right through my well-hidden sentries and walked into the village, where he was promptly knocked down, roped and lodged in a hut. In this way we collected half a dozen wild natives in a week.

"One night I heard the *ngoma* drums throbbing and beating far off in the heart of the primeval forest.

"'Machunga,' I said to the ex-convict, who had been brought to me, 'do you hear the drums?'

"'I hear them, *Bwana Mkubwa!*' he replied and I saw him shudder.

"'Now is the time that you will lead me to the place of sacrifice,' I told him.

"'Bwana, I dare not!' he answered.

"'Yet you will!' I said, and laid my revolver upon the little camp table before me.

"He eyed the weapon apprehensively for a moment.

"'It shall be as you wish,' he muttered sullenly.

"Then followed a nightmare march through the bush; Machunga went first with the muzzle of my revolver screwed into the small of his back and my left hand gripping his shoulder. Behind me followed the fifteen *asikari*, each man holding on to his comrade in front and each man carefully instructed as to what was expected of him later on.

"We seemed to have been walking through Stygian darkness for all eternity, and the maddening throb of the drums grew ever louder in our ears.

"Presently we caught a faint gleam of light among the tree trunks. Machunga stopped dead, so that I stumbled on to him and the man behind bumped into me. Then we went forward again, catching a glimpse of light one moment then losing it again altogether the next. By this time the roar of the drums was so insistent that you could not hear yourself speak.

"At last we were near enough to make out a great company of people squatted round a blazing fire. I stopped and whispered to the man behind me. The signal was passed down the line and, almost at once, I could feel men moving cautiously to left and right of me through the dense undergrowth. Luckily the noise of the drums covered our movements. Suddenly the beating ceased; there was a silence that felt as if you could cut it with a knife.

"I crept forward to the edge of the clearing, gripping Machunga tightly by the shoulder.

"The silence lasted a full moment, then the drum-beaters started to ply their sticks once more and slowly the whole assembly began to move, swaying gently—shuffle to the right, shuffle to the left and a quick leap forward. At the head of the circling procession crept, danced and gesticulated the *wachawi* (the witch-doctors) looking like the fiends of hell they were.

"As suddenly as the drumming had commenced it ceased again. All the dancers sank down upon their heels in a circle. Then I saw that which had been hidden from me before and which made me catch my breath in a quickly stifled gasp.

"In the middle of the ring seventeen still forms were pegged out upon the ground; the centre figure was that of a white man—

the District Commissioner of Kema. At his feet, stretched at right angles, was his native servant."

Logan paused for a moment in his narrative, picked up the curiously curved knife from the Moorish coffee stool and weighed it upon the palm of his hand.

"Before I could make any movement," Bruce continued, "the chief witch-doctor leaped forward with this knife gleaming in his hand. The glow of the firelight made it appear to be already stained with blood. Stooping swiftly down he slashed the wretched servant who lay at the Commissioner's feet across the throat.

"'The white man who comes has found new eyes,' he screamed; 'with this man's life shall pass his vision.'

"I felt Machunga tremble violently and the sweat break out upon his body beneath my hand. He realised fully that the man newly dead represented him in the drama.

"The witch-doctor was standing upright again now with the bloody knife held high above his head and his legs astride the body of the Commissioner.

"'The white man's life shall pass with the life of his kind!' he yelled, and the foam flew from his frenzied lips.

"But I didn't wait for any more horrors. My revolver was covering the brute and now I pressed the trigger. The heavy bullet took him fairly between the eyes and he went down, kicking convulsively, upon the Commissioner's body.

"Then pandemonium broke loose. My men opened rapid fire in accordance with their orders and, in less than five minutes, the clearing was like a shambles. Some of the natives broke through our ring and escaped it is true, but the majority threw down their weapons and awaited the end in sullen silence. The moment the spears, shields, knives and clubs clattered down I sounded my whistle for the 'Cease Fire.'

"After we had released the Commissioner—and a mightily relieved man he was—and his fellow victims, we roped our prisoners together and waited for the dawn.

"At daybreak we returned to the village. There the Commissioner and I constituted ourselves into a court of two and hanged the chief out of hand. His councilors and the witch-doctors the Commissioner decided should be flogged and sent to gaol. The rest of the male population I 'recruited' for the Military Labour Corps. The village we set on fire before we left.

"Oh yes! and there was one other thing I meant to tell you. While we were waiting for dawn at the place of sacrifice I got Machunga to show me the spot at which he said the week-old child had been buried. My men opened up the ground with the big eighteen-inch chopping knives—'*pangas*' we call them—which they carry. There, sure enough, we found the remains of a baby. But the rain and the insects had so destroyed the corpse that it was impossible to say whether or not the eyes had been put out, the ears deafened, and the lips sewn up.

"Still, I often wonder what would have happened if Machunga had not taken it into his head to come along to my camp that night after the sentry had been murdered."

* * * * * *

Logan got up and walked across the room; he replaced the curved knife among the trophies which adorned his walls.

"Ugh!" exclaimed Jack Spenser, "you've spoiled my chances of a night's sleep; confound you, Bruce!"

III
THE POWER OF THE SPIRIT

Captain Bruce Logan was leaning against the mantelpiece in the study of his house in Regent's Terrace, contemplating the portrait of a thin-faced man, upon whose features the East had stamped its indelible record. Hugh Trent, clad as usual in his host's old velvet smoking jacket lounged in a corner of the big Chesterfield drawn close to the fire. Jack Spenser, who had accompanied his two friends to a disappointing lecture concerning "Life after Death," wandered aimlessly about the room, inspecting the many heads and trophies hung upon the walls, which bore silent witness to Logan's world-wide wanderings. After a while he turned to the fire and sat down beside Trent.

"It's all very well, you know, for that lecturer fellow to talk about the sub-conscious mind and faked spirit photographs," he said, "but how do you account for all these marvelous messages that are coming through, telling us the exact nature of the Hereafter?"

"I don't know," said Trent; "but it seems to me that the revelations are no more wonderful than the discovery of, say, wireless telegraphy, or any other new force. It is, in my opinion, all a matter of progress and change. Particularly the latter, for as we lose through disuse some of our faculties so we acquire others to compensate for them. For example, we, with our greater facilities for mechanical communication, have almost entirely lost the art of telepathy which we undoubtedly once possessed and which is manifested in an extraordinary degree, I understand, by certain of the more primitive native peoples to this very day. But upon this question of soul projection, or whatever you care to term it, I dare not speak authoritatively in the presence of Bruce, who has lived so long in the East. What is your opinion upon the question, old fellow?" he added, turning to Bruce Logan, who still leaned against the mantelpiece with the photograph of the thin-faced man in his hands.

Bruce smiled reminiscently, and again looked long at the portrait.

"Is it telepathy you have in mind?" he asked.

"Something of that sort, I fancy," replied Trent.

"Yes," said Jack Spenser. "It was what is called telepathy that I had in mind when I spoke."

"In that case," said Bruce Logan, "your argument is sound so far, at all events, as the people of the East are concerned, for they have the power in a peculiarly pronounced degree. It seems, however, to be used differently in various parts of the world."

"How do you mean 'differently'?" queried Spenser.

"Well, in India, for example," answered Bruce, "the effort is quite a conscious one; the native enters into a state of trance before projecting his spirit. But the West Africans have less need to use the power, since they have perfected a system of signaling by means of the *lokali*—a small drum—the top of which is beaten with a pair of ironwood sticks. This *lokali* is a peculiarly efficient form of bush telegraph. In East and parts of Central Africa, however, the telepathic spirit is abnormally developed, or rather has lost little of its original power. For instance, towards the end of the German East African campaign, one battalion of the 3rd Regiment King's African Rifles was badly cut up at Nammacurru on the Quilimane River. None of the *asikari*—native soldiers—were conscious of projecting a message, of that I am convinced; and yet their comrades in Nairobi, many hundreds of miles to the north, knew of the disaster two or three hours before the news had been conveyed by telegraph to headquarters."

Bruce Logan paused for a moment, as if considering the advisability of amplifying his statement.

"I believe, under certain circumstances, the power may be acquired by a white man out of sympathy with his kind and closely associated with a native."

"That's extraordinarily interesting," said Spenser, "but how is it brought about?"

"Wasn't it Kipling who said: 'Let the white go to the white and the black to the black. Then whatever trouble falls is in the ordinary course of things'?" Logan asked, as he walked over and seated himself in his deep armchair.

"Yes," answered Trent, taking a cigarette from a silver box which stood upon the Moorish coffee-stool set at his elbow. "It is his prelude to a particularly unpleasant story. Why?"

"I was only thinking," said Logan, "of an incident which had a distinctly spiritualistic touch, although not in any way connected with the 'Life after Death' business which appears to be bothering Jack."

"What's the yarn, Bruce?" asked Trent in his blunt manner.

Logan laid the photograph down upon his knee and reached for a rhinoceros-foot box containing his black Boer tobacco; he slowly filled the big meerschaum pipe, which had come undamaged through his many wanderings and various adventures. When the tobacco was burning to his satisfaction, he again picked up the portrait.

"This fellow, Henry Warren," he said, "was just about as psychic as anyone I ever knew and, incidentally, he disbelieved absolutely in the whole business. I met him out in Zanzibar a good many years ago. He was not exactly a favourite with the white population, but that, I fancy, was because he understood too much about native affairs for the comfort of certain of his brother officials. He took too much interest in the native question altogether.

"Zanzibar is a picturesque place enough, even from the tourist's point of view. To the man who knows sufficient to see below the surface, its possibilities are unlimited.

"Africa was everything to Warren, so dear, indeed, that I am quite sure he could never have lived long in any other country. I remember on one occasion he was granted six months' leave to England; at the end of three months he was back again in Zanzibar, having heard that the Government were to try a new policy for the Island of Pemba.

"As it happened, the town was pretty full at the time of his return. His bungalow was occupied by another official, who could not very well be dispossessed, wherefore Warren came along and shared my quarters. That is how I happen to know the story I am going to tell you. I have been at some pains to substantiate and complete it by interrogating the other people who were concerned.

"Warren, who spoke Swahili, Arabic and Hindustani fluently, always insisted upon buying our food himself, which is not precisely the European custom out there.

"One morning we were down in the *sukoni*—or native market, as I suppose you would call it—Warren had just completed our purchases and we were making our way through the throng, when an Arab in a voluminous camel-hair robe sidled up and whispered something in his ear. I saw Warren start and observe the man closely. He gripped the fellow by the arm and asked him several questions in so low a voice that I could not catch their import.

"Back at the bungalow Warren sat silent over his lunch, apparently turning something over and over in his mind. Once or twice I looked up and caught him regarding me speculatively. When the 'boys,' after bringing in our coffee on to the verandah, had retired to their own quarters, he leant across the little table which stood between us.

"'Logan,' he said, 'we've been pretty good pals since you came out here; you are, indeed, the only real friend I have in the place. Would you back me up in a rather curious adventure if I asked your help?'

"I told him that I was game for anything in reason and at that we left it.

"Two days later he came to my room, just as I was preparing for bed. He had a couple of camel-hair robes, dyed black, such as the Arabs wear, thrown over his arm, and in his hand he held two thin, wicked-looking knives in leather sheaths.

"He threw the clothes and 'cutlery' upon my bed and sat down in a long chair.

"'You remember what I said to you after lunch two days ago?' he asked. In answer to my murmur of confirmation, he continued:

'There is to be a sale of slaves at Ahmed Hamel's to-night, and I think that the Government should be represented.'

"Although I smiled at the matter-of-fact way in which he conveyed this surprising information, I must admit that I awaited somewhat apprehensively his next words.

"'If you were serious in what you promised last Wednesday,' he said, 'slip on the *ngamia* robe and stick one of those knives into your belt. It might also be as well to put an automatic pistol in your breeches pocket,' he added as an afterthought.

"I did as he requested, and asked what was to happen next.

"He led me by devious ways through narrow winding streets to the Arab quarter of the old town. We paused before one of those curious spike-studded doors, of which so few now remain, thanks to the American visitors. At this door he knocked sharply, in a peculiar manner, with his knife hilt. It swung silently open, to admit us to a long, dark corridor, down which we were led by a big Nubian, black as Eblis.

"At the end of the corridor another door opened upon a courtyard thronged with people squatting about a platform and a small rostrum, before which a great fire blazed.

"We made our way into the crowd and squatted down on our heels in native fashion. I looked about me beneath the shadow of my hood, studying the assembly. There were light-skinned Swahilis, jet-black Nubians; Arabs, Hindoos and more than a sprinkling of Greeks—all gazing stolidly towards the platform. No one spoke!

"Suddenly there was a crash of barbaric music. The big Nubians employed by Ahmed Hamel pushed and drove the front ranks of the audience back into a wider circle as half-a-dozen naked Zanzibari girls danced out into the firelight. This was evidently to be a prelude to the proper proceedings of the evening. The girls whirled and twisted, with the leaping firelight flashing from their sinuously moving limbs; and still the audience made no sign. At last the dancers flung themselves panting upon the hard-beaten earth. There was no applause. I remember a Hindoo close to me continued indifferently munching betel-nut, the juice of which had long since stained his teeth, lips and beard a brilliant scarlet.

"As the Nubians herded the dancing girls away, Ahmed Hamel stepped lithely on to the rostrum beside the platform. At last a little thrill of anticipation seemed to run through the waiting audience. I felt Warren stir beside me, but when I looked at him his eyes, which I could just see beneath the shadow of his hood, were staring stolidly in front of him.

"Ahmed treated us to the usual auctioneer's patter of expatiation upon the excellence of the 'goods' to be offered and which, he said, had been brought from the interior and 'elsewhere' secretly and at great risk and expense.

"The first three women put up on the platform were the usual type of black *bibi*, two of them woolly-haired and generally negroid in appearance; the third a thin, regular-featured Nandi, with straight, black hair. These three 'lots' were disposed of quickly at low prices.

"There was a pause in the proceedings, a slight scuffle in the dark background, the musical chink of gold anklets, before a slim form, heavily veiled and thickly cloaked, was pushed up on to the platform.

"A Nubian stood back, sulkily nursing a bleeding hand which the girl had bitten. Ahmed leaned forward from his perch.

"'Take off that veil!' he commanded harshly.

"The girl made no movement of compliance. Ahmed leaned forward and, grasping the gauzy wrapping in his strong hand, rent it roughly from the girl's head and shoulders.

"I gave a gasp of wonder as the veil fell away, for the woman's flesh shone like minted gold in the gleaming firelight. She could not have been more than sixteen years of age and was almost white. Her limbs were delicately moulded and a great cloud of silky hair hung in rippling waves to her waist. Her feet and hands were tiny, light as lotus leaves, to rest in the palm of a man's one hand. She might have owned to any nationality, from Spanish to Cingalese; she was, as we subsequently learned, a high caste Hindoo.

"The bidders and buyers stirred interestedly at sight of her.

"A Greek started the bidding at a hundred rupees, whereat old Ahmed smiled sarcastically, until an Arab immediately capped it with two hundred. After that the bidding went briskly forward, until a thousand rupees was offered by the Arab. Then Warren spoke.

"'Fifteen hundred,' he said quietly in Arabic.

"'Two thousand,' shouted the Arab.

"'Three,' replied Warren and at that figure the girl was knocked down to him. By this time my fingers were closing round the butt of my automatic, for I was feeling pretty anxious. Warren, however, seemed quite unperturbed. Getting leisurely to his feet he strolled across to the platform. Taking the girl by the chin, he tilted up her face as if he wished to examine more closely his purchase. He spoke to her in Hindustani, bidding her put on her veil; then murmured something in her ear so low that its meaning was for her alone; but I saw her eyes flash upwards to his face.

"Once clear of Ahmed's premises, I turned to Warren and asked him what he proposed doing with the girl.

"'I don't know,' he said. 'For the present we will lodge her with Musa bin Mahommed; after that we shall see, perhaps I may be able to find out to whom she belongs.'

"Next morning a strange Arab came to my bungalow asking for Warren by name—a most unusual thing for a native to do. He was brought to us on the verandah. A fine strapping fellow I had never seen in Zanzibar before.

"'What do you want?' I asked him in Swahili.

"'My business is with Warren Effendi,' he answered in tolerably good English.

"Warren took him up sharply in Arabic, for he held strong views as to the natives using the white man's tongue.

"'State your business in your own language,' he commanded.

"'*Iwa*, Effendi,' said the fellow. 'Last night you visited Ahmed Hamel's.'

"'Well,' queried Warren, 'what of it?'

"'You bought a woman there, Effendi; she is mine,' said the Arab.

"'How do you mean, she is yours?' asked Warren.

"'She has been mine ever since I took her in India,' replied the man, 'and, but for the meanness of my brother, upon whom be the brand of the dog because he did not buy her last night, would be mine even now.'

"'That you stole her from her home does not alter the fact that I bought her,' said Warren.

"'I will give you double the price you paid,' said the Arab.

"'Not if you offered me ten times the price,' replied Warren.

"'Very well,' said the other. 'But guard her well, Effendi, for I, Ibrahim bin Hassan, have sworn to have her, and my word has never yet been broken.'

"Warren was about to reply angrily, when the Arab turned and stalked down the steps and across the compound to the street.

"'Well, of all the damned impudence!' said Warren. 'But the fellow is right, and I shall take his advice and have the girl carefully guarded for so long as she is in my care.'

"'So you think he is really dangerous, Warren?' I queried.

"'Hum!' said Warren. 'They say that the Corsican is a pretty good hand at carrying on a vendetta, but you touch one of these Arabs on the raw—particularly where women are concerned—and you are in for a blood feud beside which any European quarrel is but the merest child's play.'

"'Under these circumstances I suppose that you will get rid of the girl at the earliest possible moment?' I suggested.

"'I'm not sure,' answered Warren. 'Ibrahim has set me thinking, and I must find out more about her. She seems to be a person of some importance.'

"'Better leave the affair alone and get shot of her,' I grumbled.

"But I might as well have saved my breath, for it would be just about as useful to try to stop a charging rhino with a bullet from a Service revolver as to attempt to turn Warren from his purpose once his mind was made up. For the better part of a week he debated the problem, while diligent inquiry was being made through his own private and peculiar sources.

"Then it was that he made a bad mistake—that of seeing the girl again. Her name was Azizun and, as I had half anticipated, she was from India, whence she had been carried away by Ahmed's emissaries.

"From the first day that he saw her Warren loved Azizun. It was no case of a rose-bud love blooming to maturity slowly, but a sudden flaming passion which changed the whole of existence for him. There was a peculiarly subtle significance in the whole affair.

"He, who hitherto had studied the natives dispassionately, realised that he was ready to pour out all the passion of his soul upon the lips of a coloured woman.

"I'm convinced that, for awhile, he fought the temptation with all the strength that was in him. But strength of that sort doesn't last overlong in the tropics, and Warren was not quite normal in those days; nearly all the men-folk of Zanzibar kept aloof from him and the women held him at arm's length.

"He grew more morose each day and went more often at night to the house of Musa bin Mahommed.

"As is too often the case where native women are concerned, Azizun, as I have already said, had conceived a violent attachment to the white man who had befriended her. She besought him not to send her back to India, saying that her caste had been destroyed irretrievably by her capture by the Arabs, for which reason her own people would not be willing to receive her back into their home.

"Soon there began a double life, which any sane man must have known could only end in tragedy and unhappiness. In the first place, the native girl matures to womanhood more quickly than does her Western sister; enjoys no middle age and declines into queasy old age when white women are still in their prime. Secondly, when East meets West, there is always to be faced the awful problem of the half-caste children, whose lot is the most pitiful in the whole world. And, apart from these considerations, there was always the menacing shadow of Ibrahim bin Hassan and his sworn vengeance lurking in the background of their lives.

"Warren did not shut his eyes to these facts, he simply ignored them and went contentedly upon his own headstrong way, heedless alike to advice and entreaty, although, God knows, I plagued him enough with both.

"Day by day he got through his office work, attended Government functions and paid such duty calls as it was impossible to avoid. Night by night he slipped on his black camel-hair robe and strolled away to the house of Musa, where Azizun was still lodged. No other white man except myself knew of this hidden life which was dearer than anything else in the world to him.

"His delight in it all I can well understand, for he was an intensely lonely man, who hid an infinite capacity for affection; a man without a niche of his own in our Zanzibar society, totally incomprehensible to his fellow whites—except possibly myself— and as little comprehending their views. And to such, the peace, understanding and tender ministrations he found at Azizun's hands in Musa's dwelling must have been a complete and all-sufficient paradise.

"I have no doubt that he would have married Azizun, but that he knew, as every man knows who has lived in the East, that nothing but unhappiness can come of such mixed marriages. Despite his knowledge, I believe that the thought of marriage was present in his mind, for a time at all event, for he taught Azizun to speak, write, and read English and had her baptised a Christian.

"Then came a time when he was sent on a mission to Pemba. He did not like going a little bit and made me swear by all that I held holy that I would see Azizun or Musa every day to find out that all was well. He never seemed to forget the threat made by Ibrahim bin Hassan that he would again carry off the girl.

"His fears were well founded, for Ibrahim did try while Warren was away to gain admittance to the house where Azizun was, but old Musa warned him off pretty savagely, I fancy.

"When Warren returned some months later he was a mere bag of bones, a total wreck from repeated attacks of malaria. The doctors at once ordered him to England, but he would not go until Azizun added her word to others and he was thus overpersuaded.

"The night before the ship sailed he went as usual to the house of Musa. I went to his room when he returned, and, as he was changing his clothes, I noticed that the little crucifix which always hung about his neck was missing. Knowing how greatly he valued the talisman, I asked if he had lost it.

"'No,' he replied, 'I have given it to Azizun, perhaps it may guard her from harm. And you, Bruce, you will look after her for me, won't you? I have told her she is to send for you if she wants anything.'

"I told him that he need have no fear, and he remained silent until he had finished dressing. Suddenly he wheeled round and faced me.

"'Bruce, old fellow,' he said, 'that girl is more than my life to me. If she called to me, all across the world, I believe that I should hear and answer.'"

* * * * * *

For a while Logan sat quietly thinking, then rose and mixed himself a whisky and soda.

"What was the end of it all?" asked Spenser. "I can see that the yarn is not yet finished."

Logan thought for a moment longer.

"Warren came home to England," he said, "and went straight into hospital. He was pretty bad, for he had developed dysentery on the boat coming over, and that, on the top of malaria, very nearly finished him.

"One night when Nurse Holton, a girl who had more insight, or perhaps had suffered more than her sisters, was making her rounds of the darkened wards she came to Warren's bed and found him wakeful.

"'Can't you sleep, Mr. Warren?' she asked.

"'No, Sister,' he answered; 'something from Africa seems to be calling me. I feel as if I was badly needed out in Zanzibar to-night.'

"She sat down beside him.

"'Won't you tell me about it?' she asked. 'Perhaps if you talked a little it would ease your mind, and then you could get to sleep.'

"For a moment Warren hesitated, fighting against his natural reserve. Then an instinctive understanding of the nurse's sympathy must have come to him, for he told her, freely and openly, the story of his life out in Zanzibar with Azizun.

"'And I gave her my mother's crucifix,' he concluded. 'I told her that if she called I would come from the ends of the earth—'

"He stopped suddenly and started up on to his elbow, staring intently down the ward.

"In the dim light the nurse saw his muscles stiffen and become tense. Suddenly he thrust his open hand in front of him, as if striving to push someone away.

"'What is the matter?' she whispered.

"But Warren did not answer.

"He was gazing down the ward and his face was set, like an angry mask.

"'Ibrahim, thief!' he snarled.

"The harsh gutturals of the Arabic tongue rang through the ward, awakening the other patients.

* * * * * *

"That same night out in Zanzibar I was roused out of my bed by a terrific noise from the 'boys" quarters.

"'You cannot see the Bwana, he is asleep,' I heard my head-boy expostulate.

"'I tell you I must and will see him,' another voice exclaimed.

"'Who are you to awaken the Bwana Mkubwa from his sleep?' demanded my boy.

"'I am Musa bin Mahommed,' came the answer.

"By that time I had pulled on mosquito boots over my pyjamas and was searching for a dressing gown.

"'Let Musa wait,' I shouted. 'I will be there in a moment.'

"Shortly afterwards the old Arab was brought to me in the dining-room.

"'What is the matter, Musa?' I asked.

"'Effendi,' he replied, 'to-night the thief Ibrahim broke into my house, and now lies dead in Azizun's room.'

"Waiting only to snatch up a heavy camel-hair cloak, into the pocket of which I slipped my automatic, I hurried with Musa to his dwelling. On arrival there he took me straight to Azizun's room, where I found her lying upon the bed, prostrate with fright.

"'Oh, sahib,' she cried, 'you have come at last!'

"'Why, what has happened?' I asked.

"'To-night,' she told me, 'Ibrahim bin Hassan burst in the window and seized me as I slept upon my bed. He put his hand upon my mouth to prevent me from crying out. He commenced to carry me towards the open window. I struggled desperately and broke free from him.

"'When he turned to seize me again I lifted up the talisman my lord had placed about my neck at parting and called upon the sahib's God. Ibrahim laughed and told me that Mahomet was the stronger prophet; but I called to *Ahre* and his God to save me. Then a voice cut like a whip-lash across the silence of the room. "Ibrahim, thief!" cried the voice, and Ibrahim stood still, staring with frightened eyes. Then I saw my lord, in a long white robe and looking—oh, so ill! He stretched out his hand and pushed Ibrahim back, and, at my lord's touch, Ibrahim seemed to crumple up.'

"When Azizun had finished her story, and I had questioned her a little, I went over to look at Ibrahim where he lay, just below the open window.

"The face was set in a mask of rigid terror. I opened his burnous, and there, just above the heart, I saw the livid marks of five fingers and the palm of a man's hand."

* * * * * *

Bruce looked thoughtfully at the bowl of his big meerschaum pipe for a moment or two, as he waited for the full significance of the story to sink into his hearers' brains.

"'There are more things in heaven and earth,'" quoted Hugh Trent softly.

"Yes, I thought that, too," said Bruce. "That was why I sent Harry Warren a cable next morning to tell him that everything was all right in Zanzibar."

IV
OUT OF THE BEYOND

I

JACK SPENSER, with his unconquerable taste for the unusual, was apt to meet with some curious experiences.

Spiritualism was his ruling passion at the moment.

On the afternoon in question he had attended a *séance* at which a new, but already famous, medium was present.

No "adjuncts of mystery" had been used: the purpose of the people concerned being to obtain a materialisation. They had been successful beyond their wildest dreams and the spirit which had materialised was that of Spenser's younger brother, Tom, killed by a German sniper in the Ypres salient three years ago.

Jack's dilettante interest had been shaken from its foundations and he now felt like a man standing upon the brink of an unfathomable abyss into which something precious has been hurled.

He stood upon the kerbstone dazed and hardly knowing what to think. After a further moment he raised his hand to a crawling taxi and before getting in gave the driver the address of Bruce Logan's house in Regent's Terrace.

Entering the study unannounced he found Logan and Hugh Trent reclining in two chairs drawn close to a roaring fire of logs, for it was a bitter November evening. Between them stood a Moorish coffee stool bearing a big silver tray of tea things.

"Come along," said Logan, looking up, "you're just in time for some tea. But I don't think, knowing Hugh's capacity for tea-cake and muffins, that he will welcome you as he would have done an hour later."

"What a horrible libel," laughed Trent, then turning to Spenser, he added: "Well, Jack, how did the magic mystery pan out this time? Get a manifestation of Caesar's ghost or anything interesting?"

"Don't rot, old man," replied Jack. "It was my brother's spirit which materialised." There was an uncomfortable silence for a moment, then Trent stuck out his chin in an uncompromising manner which the men of his platoon in France had always recognised as a sign of "seeing things through in the face of odds."

"Look here, Jack," he said. "I don't want you to think me an unfeeling brute, but I do want to get this matter straight. Half the world seems to be running mad nowadays, trying to get into touch with dead relations. I admit that the desire is a perfectly natural one, but I can't believe in this materialisation business. I've seen too many good men blown to fragments or pounded to pulp to believe in it, that's all."

"But, man alive," replied Jack excitedly, "I saw Tom. I tell you I saw him as plainly as I see you sitting there."

"Right," said Hugh; "I'm quite willing to believe that you saw him, or at, any rate, thought you did; but tell me this: he was shot through the head, wasn't he?"

"He was."

"Very well, then, did you see any mark of the bullet wound when you believed you saw him this afternoon?"

"No, I didn't."

"That, to my mind, settles it."

At this point Bruce Logan intervened. "You have believed the tales of the East I have told you from time to time?" asked Bruce.

"Yes, of course; why do you ask?" came the instant reply.

"Because an incident occurs to my mind which might interest you," said Bruce. "Shall I tell you the story?"

"By all means let us have it," Hugh replied, settling himself more comfortably in his deep chair and lighting a cigarette.

"Very well," said Bruce. "I think, some time ago, when I told you of my adventures on the Island of Kema, I promised some day to tell you of how I went back to the strange people, after the Curse of the Lion had fallen upon poor Tom Harden. That is the story I propose telling you now.

"When I was stationed at Zanzibar—shortly after that affair of Harry Warren's, to be precise—I was lent to the Egyptian Government for awhile for special duty at Alexandria. I was not best pleased at the change, for the officials, natives and everyone else were of a different stamp from those to whom I had grown accustomed, nor did the essentially French character of the city suit my taste. I became a member of the Victoria Club in Old Bourse Street, however, and made the best of things.

"One night I saw a stranger in the Club picking up papers in a desultory sort of way which indicated that he was at a loose end and pretty bored with life. I went over to where he was standing by the centre table in the end room and offered him a drink. Then we sat down and chatted upon general topics for a while. The man who had introduced that stranger to the Club and promised to meet him there didn't mature, so I asked him to dine with me.

"Curiously enough we sat at the same table at which poor Tom Harden and I had dined in 1902, the night he suggested that I should go to Africa on a big-game hunting expedition with him.

"My new-found friend's name was Smithson—Hulbert Smithson. He was a tall, fine-looking fellow, with a big, blonde moustache and fierce blue eyes set in a sun-bronzed face. I fancy he was an American, although he never told me so and I never asked him. He had fought in every war and under pretty well every flag for the last fifteen years and knew the world as well as a billiard marker knows the back of his left hand.

"Naturally enough the conversation turned to Africa, the most mysteriously attractive country in the world.

"Smithson apparently had thoroughly enjoyed the Boer war and had lately supplemented his fighting experiences and added to his medals by taking part, with the 3rd King's African Rifles, in the expedition led by Major Pope Hennessey against the Sotik tribe.

"'When I was down at Kericho, in the Kisumu Province, towards the end of the show last July,' he said, 'I picked up some information from a strange native, of no known tribe, which set me wondering. It's taken me the best part of a year to get that "boy's" story more or less substantiated and the result is, to say the least of it, interesting.'

"I asked him what the yarn was, but he seemed to feel that he had been talking too freely to a stranger and wouldn't say any more.

"'Tell me about your own African adventures,' he said, with the obvious intention of changing the conversation.

"'Curiously enough,' I replied, 'my adventures started at this very table when I dined with a man called Tom Harden, nearly four years ago.'

"Then I told him how we had gone north from Nairobi to get an okapi; how we had come to the country of the Strange People and how, after Tom had shot the tribal lion deity, the Tree Wizard had put the Curse of the Lion upon him, which had resulted in his death at the London Zoological Gardens.

"As I told the tale his eyes opened wider and wider; when I came to the part about the 'Elephants' Grave Yard,' he couldn't contain himself any longer.

"'Why, why!' he burst out. 'You mean to say you have been there and have actually seen the ivory?'

"'Yes,' I replied, 'why does that surprise you so greatly?'

"'Damn it all, man,' he exclaimed, 'that's the very thing the native told me about at Kericho—the "Elephants' Grave Yard." Do you realise that you are the only living white man who has ever seen it? I've been more than a year searching for anyone who could tell me anything at all and then to think that I should accidentally stumble across you, who have actually been there, here in this club. Good Lord! I can hardly believe it.'

"'Yes, but why are you so interested?' I asked.

"'Why, because I've been more than a month negotiating with the Soudanese Government to lead an expedition up to get the stuff, but they couldn't make up their minds to risk the necessary outlay because they thought I hadn't enough knowledge to carry the show through, or even to be absolutely sure that the stuff is there. Now you just happen along and solve the whole problem as easy as rolling off a log. Of course, you'll go with me?' he asked anxiously.

"'I'd like to,' I replied, 'but I'm here on Government service, lent for a specific job by my boss at Zanzibar.'

"'Oh, that's all right,' he answered; 'leave the different departments to wrangle it out amongst themselves. They'll fix it all right, if you're willing to come.'

"To cut a long story short Smithson seemed to have some sort of pull. He worked like a maniac and managed to get matters adjusted to his liking in a most miraculous manner.

"The end of it all was that, at the end of a month, we found ourselves on a boat bound up the Nile, having departed twenty-four hours previously with twenty Soudanese soldiers, armed but not in uniform, and an official assurance that if we got ourselves into trouble we must get ourselves out again, as the Government could accept no responsibility for us. This rather amused me, considering the fact that I had been 'lent' for the expedition, which was, moreover, financed from Government funds; however, I don't think the risk worried either of us much, one way or the other."

II

"It is not necessary to describe our journey up the Nile, for it was entirely uneventful.

"Things went so smoothly at first, and for long after we left the river, in fact, that I began to fear that big trouble would trip us up sooner or later. Nor was I wrong in my apprehensions.

"We had been marching for many days through the Tirkanaland wastes and were rapidly approaching our objective when misfortune came upon us. Several times during our more recent marches we had seen in the distance natives of a tribe to which neither Smithson nor I could give a name. Seen through our binoculars these men appeared to be tall, finely built, very light in colour and of a markedly European cast of countenance. They, however, carried the usual equipment of the native warrior, that is to say, large buffalo hide shields and heavy, long-bladed spears. A Somali cattleherd, whom we met and questioned, told us these men belonged to the Ajibu tribe. The name puzzled me considerably, for it means, in the Swahili tongue, 'he answers.' He told us further that they were very fierce and that no white man had ever entered their land and left it again alive.

"One morning I awakened just before dawn and shouted for my 'boy,' Hamesi Ali, to bring tea. He did not appear with his usual celerity and I called again, angrily, to know why he had not answered. A second later the flap of my tent was torn rudely aside and instead of the jet-black countenance and slight figure of my Soudanese servant there appeared an Ajibu warrior who might well have been a Greek dressed up as a native, so light was his skin and so aquiline his features. He stood still a moment regarding me, and then, as I attempted to rise, he hurled himself forward, pinning me down beneath the mosquito net, which completely prevented me from defending myself. As he held me down he gave a high, wailing cry which was instantly answered and interrupted by an uproar of shouting. I struggled violently to throw him off, but the point of his spear pressed against my throat quickly quieted me and I lay still, wondering what would happen next.

"I had not long to wait. Five minutes later half a dozen European-looking savages entered the tent and dragged me from my bed, after which they bound my arms securely behind me and led me outside. There I found Smithson similarly trussed up and swearing like a trooper in a dozen different languages, but failing to elicit any response from our captors. Our servants, soldiers, and porters were all herded together and overawed by a ring of spearmen who looked only too willing to use their weapons but I noticed with considerable satisfaction that the Soudanese had been allowed to retain their rifles, nor was any attempt made, either then or afterwards, to take Smithson's and my revolvers from us.

"'Here's a go,' shouted Smithson the moment he caught sight of me. 'What in hell do the fellows want? I've cursed them in every language I can think of; I've offered them ransom, all our trade goods, or a share in the profits, but I can't get them to open their silly mouths for anything. Who the devil are they, anyway?'

"I told him that I was as much in the dark as he was, and then myself tried questioning the leader in every African dialect of which I had any knowledge. It was all to no purpose, he simply would not answer.

"Presently my captor said something to his comrades in a tongue remarkably like the jargon I have heard spoken by the Jews in Palestine and in the East End of London.

"At his word we were forced into line and driven forward into the bush. We crashed along through the undergrowth for the best part of two hours before emerging upon a broad and beautifully built roadway, which ran straight as an arrow through the forest. This road we followed for another hour and then entered a big township. Evidently the poorer quarter lay upon the outskirts, for the men and women, who swarmed out to see us, were barefooted and clad only in the scanty girdle of the African savage. And very strange it was to see people of European appearance thus dressed, or perhaps I should say, undressed.

"As we marched into the town the whole character of the people and place changed. The men and women were clad in long, flowing garments, rather like the *khanzoos* the African house-boys wear; the well-kept streets intersected each other at right angles, but the houses surprised me most, for there was no suggestion of the hut of the savage about them; they were log built, foursquare, with high doors and roofed with logs at a steep pitch overlaid with large leaves.

"After a while we came to a big house standing at the side of what appeared to be the central square upon which all the streets converged.

"Outside this building we waited for some time before an old man with a long grey beard came out and stood lost in contemplation of us.

"'Seems to me,' whispered Smithson, 'that we've found the lost tribe of Israel. This is probably the high priest.'

"I did not answer him, for at that moment the old man came forward and stood stroking his beard; apparently taking in every detail of our appearance and attire. Our black servants seemed to be beneath his notice. After a while he waved his hand and, turning, walked into his dwelling. We were thereupon led to the other side of the square and locked in a big empty room. Our arms were unloosed and food was brought to us, but we were entirely ignorant of the fate of Hamesi Ali and our other followers.

"An inspection of the food provided led us to believe these curious people to be vegetarians.

"'Thank goodness they don't seem to be cannibals,' said Smithson, who was irrepressibly cheerful despite the awkward fix in which we found ourselves and the sinister stories the Somali had told.

"What troubled me was that so far no one had addressed us and the only language we had heard spoken was the jargon which, to my ear, sounded very much like Yiddish.

"The night passed uneventfully, but the following morning warriors entered and beckoned me to follow them. Smithson rose at the same time, but they motioned him back; when he stepped forward to accompany me they thrust him unceremoniously into the room and banged the door. I could hear him hammering upon the woodwork as they led me out across the square.

"As you may well imagine, I did not at all like the turn events were taking.

"Outside the patriarch's dwelling I found a large company of warriors waiting, nor had I any great difficulty in recognising them as belonging to the tribe of the Tree Wizard whose land we had set out to reach. They were much darker than the Ajibu, but still not to be confused with the African natives.

"Evidently the plot was beginning to thicken.

"Without a word of explanation or direction my captors handed me over to the chief of the warriors, whom I recognised as one I had known well in the days when poor Tom Harden and I had sojourned for a while with the Strange People.

"I greeted him and he responded to my greeting, but I asked no questions, for I did not think it wise at that time.

"We marched out of the big town into the bush, through which we traveled for three days.

"Towards sundown on the third day a lone tree set upon a high hill hove in sight. As we drew nearer I could distinguish the old wizard perched among the branches, and the tribesmen assembled around the trunk. It was all just as I had seen it that first time when Harden and I visited the place and as I had pictured it a hundred times since.

"In my own mind I wondered if the old wizard was still 'seeing' dead elephants three days' march away and sending out hunters to bring in the tusks to form a fence about his own magnificent graveyard.

"I was not, however, taken near the tree, but was conducted to a hut in which I was confined and fed for twenty-four hours under guard.

"Towards midnight of the following day I saw the glare of torches gleaming redly through the thin grass walls of the hut. A moment later the mat was pulled aside from the door and a voice said simply, 'Come.' I rose and crawled out into the open. Warriors surrounded me immediately. We made our way along the path which Harden and I had followed that fateful morning when he had slain the lion-god of the tribe and the Curse of the Lion had been put upon him by the Tree Wizard.

"As we emerged from the bush I saw a little fire glowing in the mouth of the lion's cave across the clearing. We drew near, and beyond the fire I saw the Tree Wizard crouched upon his haunches inside the cave; thin hands outstretched to the tiny blaze.

"'Ha! white man,' he said; 'I smelt you out; I, the seer of elephants beyond the range of sight, I, the servant of the lion, the curser of the slayer, I saw you upon the black water, white man. I knew the purpose of your journeying, and you are here—alive!'

"To this statement I made no reply. Presently he spoke again:

"'Sit down and warm yourself,' he said, 'and we will talk.'

"I drew near and squatted down, native fashion, in front of the fire. The smoke was very thick, but still I could see his eyes blazing at me through the murk.

"With a wide gesture he waved the warriors away and soon we were alone together in the great silence, broken only by the far-off whining of a prowling hyena. Suddenly the roar of a lion shattered the silence, making the very atmosphere tremble. I shuddered.

"'Ha! the voice of my Lord the Lion awakens memories,' ejaculated the wizard with a laugh.

"The silence remained a long time unbroken.

"At last the wizard spoke again.

"'White man,' he said, 'you seek ivory. Ivory from the fence of my graveyard. Why?'

"I told him that in my country ivory was much valued for many reasons and that we had come up to buy it from him, but that we had been captured by the Ajibu tribe before we could reach his land.

"'I know,' he said; 'the Ajibu are our cousins and took you because I asked them to do so.'

"That information completely staggered me and I sat silent waiting for him to speak again.

"'I know the way of the white people,' he continued, 'how, if you desire a thing, you will never rest until it is yours. Therefore I have brought you here instead of allowing the Ajibu tribe to kill you as they wished. For if you had been slain other white men would have come to seek you and to take the sacred ivory.'

"'That is so,' I answered, wondering whither the talk was leading us.

"'But if you go back bearing ivory with you,' he said, 'will other white men come for more?'

"'No,' I answered, 'if we go back bearing enough they will be satisfied, and we will pay for what we take.'

"He thought for a long while, gazing at me through the smoke.

"'You shall have, without payment, as much as four hundred porters can carry,' he replied, 'if you will promise, by the word of your chief, that no more white men shall journey hither seeking ivory.'

"I turned this offer over in my mind for many minutes. It seemed such a tame and simple ending to our adventures and I feared a trap.

"'But why,' I asked, 'will you give us the sacred ivory, which you will not sell, and how shall we bear it home?'

"'My people shall bear it to the water,' he answered. "It will not be the sacred ivory, but tusks from our tribal treasure.'

"'And how do I know,' I asked, 'that your people, having journeyed far with us, will not kill us and, leaving the ivory by our bones, fix the guilt upon some other tribe?'

"After thinking for a while he fanned the smoke aside and fixed my eyes with his.

"'When you journeyed hither before,' he said, 'you had a friend who slew my Lord the Lion, the god of my people, upon this very spot. Upon him I placed the Curse of the Lion. Tell me, did the vengeance fall?'

"'It fell indeed,' I answered.

"'Then,' said he, 'if he who is dead returned and told you to trust my word, would you believe?'

"'Yes, I would believe and take your word,' I answered.

"'Watch then,' he said.

From the ground about him he swept up heaps of damp leaves which he threw upon the fire, muttering words which I could not understand as he did so.

"The smoke rose up from the fire pungent, dense and strangely bitter. Presently a thin blue flame shot up among the sticks, and then, as I live, I saw the spiral of smoke take shape, and the shape was that of Tom Harden. Tom, in an old battered pith helmet and a ragged bush-blouse. I don't know how long I sat there, but it seemed to me that from a nebulous 'something' my friend's form grew strong and living in the smoke. At last he turned and looked at me.

"'Bruce,' he said, and each word was in English and very plain, 'take the ivory and leave this place before the curse that caught me falls upon you also.'

"Then the vision began to fade and presently I found myself looking into the eyes of the Tree Wizard across the fire."

* * * * * *

Logan polished the bowl of his big meerschaum pipe meditatively for a moment.

"There is not much more to tell you," he said. "Within a week, Smithson and our followers joined me. It took about a month to collect the ivory. During that time we were well treated and got some excellent big-game hunting. Thereafter the old Tree Wizard, true to his word, provided us with four hundred *wapagazi*—that is to say, caravan porters—who carried our forty tons of ivory until we were able to enlist fresh carriers, who transported the stuff the rest of the way to where Smithson could take boat down the Nile. For my own part I elected to make my way back to the Uganda railway and ultimately reached Nairobi."

As Logan concluded his story he looked interrogatively at Hugh Trent.

"Well, what do you think?" he asked.

"I was wondering," replied Trent, "in what degree the manifestation of Harden's spirit was due to the conjuring powers of the old Tree Wizard. You will notice that Harden, as you appeared to see him, was clad in the only clothes with which the wizard was familiar!"

"Yes!" replied Logan, "but you must also remember that Tom spoke to me in English, a language with which the wizard was certainly not familiar, for he spoke nothing but a sort of bastard Arabic, and, possibly, the Yiddish jargon used by the Ajibu tribesmen. What is your opinion, Jack?" he added, turning to Spenser.

"I think," replied that earnest seeker after knowledge, "that there are many things at present beyond our comprehension and powers of explanation, and that it is better either to accept them with unquestioning faith or to leave them alone altogether."

At that moment there was a discreet knock at the door. Wilkins entered and switched on the lights.

"Dinner is served, sir," he announced. The three friends rose and left the study in meditative silence.

V
IN THE LAST EVENT

BRUCE LOGAN WALKED into the study of his big house in Regent's Terrace, removed his silk hat and chamois leather gloves; having placed them upon the top of his old Chinese lacquer desk, he regarded them for a moment with positive dislike.

"Wilkins!" he shouted.

"Yes, sir," answered the servant, appearing quietly.

"Wilkins, take these damned things away and bring me a coat in which I can breathe."

"Very good, sir."

A moment later Wilkins was back, bearing a ragged old shooting jacket, the sagging pockets of which bore testimony to the weight of the many cartridges they had carried.

With a sigh of relief Bruce exchanged his immaculate morning coat for the worn and weather-stained tweed. As he sank into his favourite chair Wilkins placed upon a stool beside him a great meerschaum pipe in its case and a rhinoceros-foot tobacco-jar well filled with black Boer tobacco.

He saw that his master was in the worst of bad tempers, and knew that many pipes of the pungent tobacco alone would suffice to restore him to his accustomed serenity.

"Whisky, sir?"

"What's the time?"

"Just upon six o'clock, sir."

"Right! bring me my 'sun-downer' and some quinine."

"I 'ope 'e ain't in for another go of that there malaria," muttered Wilkins to himself.

Bruce was awaiting the arrival of Spenser and his inseparable companion, Hugh Trent, who had promised to come in for dinner. He had not long to wait; he had, indeed, but finished half a pipe when Wilkins announced his two friends.

After dinner, when they sat by the study fire in the half light of a shaded desk lamp, Wilkins brought them strange liqueurs in long curiously fashioned vessels of the thinnest glass. Bruce brewed for them wonderful Turkish coffee and offered that particular brand of cigarette which serves best as an introduction for one's own pet pipe and particular blend of tobacco.

For a while they chatted idly, then a silence fell between them. Bruce filled his great meerschaum and lay back in his armchair puffing contentedly. From the depths of shadow he spoke presently.

"A remark made earlier in the evening, that 'under no circumstances is a man justified in telling a married woman that he loves her,' has brought back to my mind an incident which may interest you."

"Your stories are always worth hearing, Bruce; go ahead," said Hugh Trent, as he settled himself more comfortably in the corner of the Chesterfield.

Jack Spenser lit a fresh cigarette from the stub of the old one, but Bruce slowly refilled his pipe with black tobacco from the rhino-foot at his elbow as he collected his thoughts.

"Do you remember the tale I told you of my first visit to Kema?" he asked.

"I should rather think so," replied Jack. "I didn't sleep comfortably for a week afterwards."

Brace smiled sardonically.

"Well," he continued, "after I returned to Zanzibar from Kema I was detailed for special duty with the Intelligence Corps on account of my knowledge of the natives and their language, which I spoke fluently. After that I had more strange adventures than I am ever likely to relate to you.

"One day the General sent for me. When I arrived the Chief of Staff, the D.A.A.G., and the head of the Intelligence Department were all with him. The table, as usual, was littered from end to end with maps. The G.O.C. was evidently pretty agitated; he was worrying at his beard with both hands in a way which bade fair to pull it out by the roots any moment.

"'Good morning, Mr. Logan,' he said. 'I want to send you on a most hazardous mission; so dangerous, indeed, that I give you the option of refusing if you wish, nor shall I blame you if you see fit so to do.'

"'I shall do my best to carry through successfully whatever task you entrust to me, sir,' I replied.

"'Ah, I thought you would not fail me,' he answered. 'Now listen carefully. A week ago von Lettow despatched from his headquarters two battalions of *asikari* and a battery of machine guns. There is nothing curious in that, of course, but what is strange is that our spies can get no news of this comparatively large force; it has, in fact, disappeared as completely as if it had vanished into thin air.'

"He paused and regarded me speculatively for a moment.

"'You have a more complete knowledge of the German language and of the native dialects than any other officer in the Intelligence Corps. Do you think you can find out where those two battalions of Bosche *asikari* have gone to?' he queried.

"'I will do my best, sir,' I answered.

"'Very well,' he said, 'I give you a free hand; use your own discretion, make whatever arrangements you see fit, and take your own time. But find them! They must be found at any cost,' he added, banging his big fist upon the table to emphasise the point.

"'They shall be found, sir,' I said, with a great deal more confidence than I actually felt, for, as you will realise, to locate two battalions in the thick African bush, which stretches from the Portuguese territory across German East Africa to Nairobi, is a more difficult matter than the finding of the proverbial needle in a bundle of hay.

"Back in my quarters I sat down upon the edge of my camp bed and tried to think the matter out. After turning it over in my mind for the best part of two hours I came to the conclusion that the information I needed would be found in one place and one place only, and that was at the Bosche headquarters and nowhere else.

"Summed up it amounted to this—the two battalions obviously comprised a flying column whose activities might have been directed against the Lindi line, the line up from Port Amelia, or in half a dozen other directions. I could doubtless have found out all about it from native sources in time; but that was just it, time was the essence of the contract. The column had to be located at once.

"Having settled these points I called Mnyogi—poor Tom Harden's boy—who had been with me a good many years.

"'Mnyogi,' I said, 'we go alone to the German country to seek news; perhaps we shall not come back.'

"'*Bwana*, I am ready,' he replied. 'When do we start?'

"'To-night,' I answered.

"That night we got aboard the trolly railway which took us part of the way to the front; after that we went right up to the line in an old Ford car belonging to the supply column.

"I showed my credentials to the officer in charge of operations and inquired what German troops were opposed to him. This he was able to tell me, as a big batch of prisoners had been captured the day before, among whom, as luck would have it, were several white German officers. Of these one was just about my build and his uniform fitted me to perfection; there was, of course, no difficulty in fitting up Mnyogi with a uniform from among the captured *asikari*.

"Next night we stole past our own advanced outposts and penetrated the German lines. Our luck was right in, for we were never even challenged. Next day, by sheer brazen bluffing, we got a lift on a lorry which was going back to the German base. We dared not, however, risk arriving on it in broad daylight and, therefore, on the third afternoon we scragged the driver and slipped off into the bush, where we lay hid for four-and-twenty hours. Then we made a wide detour which enabled us to approach the headquarters camp from the opposite direction. It was a pretty big place and there were very many German officers hurrying hither and thither. Neither subterfuge nor caution seemed of any use, so I walked boldly up the main street between the huts and tents, followed closely by Mnyogi, dressed as a German officer's orderly and carrying a German rifle and equipment.

"No one took any notice of us until we ran slap into an officer wearing the same numerals as were upon my borrowed uniform. He stopped and scrutinised me closely.

"'I do not seem to remember you,' he said.

"'No,' I answered, 'I have been in hospital many months and have only recently been transferred to the 12th. What news is there from the front?'

"'The battalion has suffered heavily,' he said. 'Only this week a whole company, including the officers, was captured.'

"'Indeed,' I answered, 'that is bad news.'

"'Ah, but wait,' he said. 'Von Lettow has a surprise in store for these cursed English.'

"'What is that?' I asked.

"'You must wait, my friend,' he replied, with a laugh. 'When our new allies come you will be glad enough to see them, eh?' With which he turned upon his heel and left me.

"That remark of his about new allies set my thoughts running in a fresh direction, I began to have a hazy notion of where the two missing battalions had gone to. It was not a comforting thought, for if my surmise was correct and we could not cry check to this new move of the enemy's, the whole success of our operations in East Africa was in jeopardy.

"Later that night we did some grisly work. After mess was over I observed a number of senior officers making their way to von Lettow's headquarters. I determined to attend that conference at all costs.

"The General's hut stood alone some little distance from any other building. It was guarded by one sentry only, who paced his circular beat slowly, pausing a few minutes at back and front. When all was clear we crept to some bushes growing close to the back of the hut and waited. It was a pitch black night luckily and we could only just make out the sentry as he stood silhouetted against the meagre glow of light which penetrated the thin grass walls.

"As the man paced off to the front of the hut I whispered a word to Mnyogi. We slipped forward and lay flat on the ground in the deepest shadow. The returning sentry halted with his back to us just in front of where we lay. I pressed Mnyogi's hand and together we sprang upon the man; as I got my arm round his neck and a hand over his mouth Mnyogi grasped him by the knees. I hated what had to be done, but that did not prevent me from getting his chin into the palm of my hand; then I dragged his head slowly round and back until I heard the vertebrae snap with a horrible click—it is a useful trick a Ghurka taught me in India many years ago. I rolled the dead man into the bush and Mnyogi took up his beat. After that I lay at the back of the hut with my ear glued to the grass wall, and each word spoken inside was quite distinct. Von Lettow was speaking.

"'The flying column has reached Emari,' he said, 'and is within one day's march of the Rhodesian border. To-morrow Captain Hitson will take up the big supply column which is parked ready. He should reach Emari in a week, as the rivers are now passable; after that we shall strike, and once into Rhodesia, the Boers will join us and we shall conquer, not only here in East Africa, but from Rhodesia to the Cape as well.'

"There was a murmur of approbation and I could tell from the sounds that maps were being examined. After a while von Lettow spoke again.

"'Here is your route, Captain Hitson,' he said. 'You must get to Emari as soon as possible, for without the supplies, which but for the floods would have accompanied the flying column, Colonel Baumgartener cannot strike.'

"As Mnyogi, still doing sentry duty, came round the hut I touched his foot, together we stole away into the undergrowth.

"Time was short now, for there would, I knew, be a fine commotion when the dead sentry was discovered and yet there was much to do. I had anticipated that the surprise attack was to be made upon Rhodesia; it was, indeed, one of the things we had feared all along, for many of the Boers were disaffected and only too eager for an excuse to rise.

"It was obvious that there was no time to warn the Rhodesians, no time to get help from the British East African forces. The only chance lay in stopping the supply column and then getting safely away to warn the British frontier-post nearest to Emari. But how to do it? That was the question.

"Signing to Mnyogi to follow I crept away to where the supply column was parked, ready to move off in the morning. Luckily the big lorries were some distance from the camp and almost at the edge of the bush. Passing the sentry boldly I walked up to the first lorry and began to examine it. To my delight it carried many tins of petrol, the next two were loaded with ammunition, and the fourth with food. Taking two petrol cans apiece we opened them and poured the oil over as much of the cargo as we could reach without discovering ourselves, then we gathered other tins and drenched the vehicles themselves and yet others with which we soaked the dry grass beneath the lorries and a good deal of the surrounding ground. When all was ready we separated and set fire to the grass on either side. Then we ran for our lives into the bush, where we soon rejoined forces. The blaze was awful and the din indescribable, bugles were blowing, officers and N.C.O.s shouting orders, everyone running; then the cartridges in the lorrys began to explode which added greatly to the wild confusion, in the midst of which we made good our escape.

"Two days later I started an attack of dysentery which rapidly grew worse until, with the frontier-post but a day's march away, I was doing less than a mile an hour. Nor was Mnyogi in much better case, but he knew, as well as I did, that it was a matter of more than life and death for me to reach the British outpost without delay.

"When I could go no further he crawled away into the bush, from which he presently returned munching some roots and leaves; these seemed to have the effect of doubling him up with agony. Then he lay down and slept. When he awakened he seemed stronger, and contrived to hoist me on his back. Incredible as it may

seem he managed to keep moving for twelve hours, although growing weaker all the time. At dawn the Rhodesian frontier-post came
in sight, but Mnyogi was rolling like a drunken man and groaning
at every step. I was only half conscious and in a sweat of fear lest
he should fall before we were seen. He made it, however, and suddenly I heard a sentry shout. At that sound Mnyogi collapsed completely, pitching me forward on to my head in the dust, where I lay
with tears streaming down my face. Then I heard a familiar voice
saying: 'By gad, it's a filthy Bosche, but the poor devil seems about
all in.' At that I began to laugh, low chuckles at first, then shriek
upon shriek of hysterical mirth which emptied me of my last remaining ounce of strength.

"When I came to I was resting on a camp bed inside the block-
house and old Tony Harband, with whom I was at school, was leaning over me with his eyeglass screwed firmly in its place.

"'By gad,' he said, 'the old beggar's comin' round! Quite an old
boys' gathering, Bruce, my lad, for Jim Wardrup's doin' second in
command to me, and there's my "missus" here as well.'

"Before I could reply Jim shoved his close-cropped, square-
jawed bullet head round the door.

"'Hello Bruce,' he said, ''fraid that orderly of yours is going to
peg out. Keeps asking for you; what'd we better do about it?'

"'Have me carried to him, will you?' I said.

"'No, no,' interposed a female voice. 'Mr. Logan must not be
moved on any account; have the "boy" brought in here.'

"Then they carried in Mnyogi and laid him on the floor beside
me. There was a greyish look beneath his black skin, his eyes were
glazing and his features seemed to have shrunk.

"I managed to drop one hand over the side of the bed, and then
I felt his lips against my fingers.

"'*Bwana*,' he whispered, 'the daylight dies and my work is finished, now I go to my rest.'

"I heard a woman sob behind me, and I managed to roll my
head sideways. Mnyogi was looking up with all the good-bye he
knew how to make in his eyes. I didn't see any more because suddenly my eyes went all misty."

Bruce stopped speaking and blew his nose.

"Damn those cigarettes of yours, Jack," he said; "they sting one's eyes most infernally!"

After that he was silent for a long time. Hugh sat quietly in the corner of the Chesterfield sucking his pipe. It was Jack who broke the silence.

"I may be pretty dense," he said, "but I don't see what all this has got to do with whether it is or is not right to make love to another man's wife."

"There was never any question of that," answered Hugh; "the point was whether a man is ever justified in telling a married woman that he loves her; that is a very different matter to making love to another man's wife. Anyway, why can't you wait and let Bruce finish his yarn his own way?"

"Oh, all right!" said Jack. "Don't get stuffy about it."

Bruce stared thoughtfully into the fire, rubbing the warm bowl of an old briar pipe against the side of his nose until the wood shone as if it had been newly varnished. Finally he finished polishing the pipe upon a silk handkerchief and slipped it back into the pocket of his coat.

After a prolonged silence, which neither Hugh nor Jack seemed disposed to break, Bruce began speaking again.

"They carried Mnyogi out and buried him decently," he said, "but I did not know anything about that at the time, for I was delirious best part of twenty-four hours.

"When I began to understand things again I found myself still tucked up in the camp-bed in a corner of the central living room of the block-house.

"Something important was afoot evidently, for Tony Harband was in the middle of the room holding his wife tightly in his arms and looking down into her eyes as if he could not bear ever to let her go again. The significance of the tableau was further emphasised by the fact that he was in marching order with water-bottle, field-glasses and haversack slung; a heavy service revolver in its holster and a pouch of cartridges attached to his Sam Browne.

"'We are certain to catch the Bosche and stop him at the drift, Phyllis,' he was saying, 'but if they do break through Jim will look after you and see that you don't fall into the hands of their black soldiers; whatever happens, and if anything should go wrong in the "dust-up" Jim will see that you are sent home safely. I'm sorry you have been let in for this, old girl, but the last thing any of us anticipated was fighting up here on the Rhodesian frontier.'

"Mrs. Harband didn't seem to be able to say anything at all. When Jim Wardrup popped his ugly old mug round the doorpost Tony was busily shining his eyeglass and his wife was trying aimlessly to polish one of his brown leather buttons with her wisp of a handkerchief.

"'Detachment on parade, sir,' reported Jim, saluting his superior officer.

"'Righto!' replied Tony. 'But listen to me a minute before I take over, because I want you to get everything quite clear, old man. I'm taking seventy of the men with me to the drift by which the Bosche is bound to cross the river and we shall hold it to the last man and the last cartridge. I've sent to headquarters for help and the guns should be here inside the week, so you must contrive somehow to hold out with your fifty men if we are mopped up. The trenches here are well sited and the mines on the hill you laid yourself, so you know that they are in order. Remember, Jim,' he whispered, leaning forward and gripping his comrade's arm, 'the Bosche has promised that every British woman captured shall be given to the *asikari*, so keep your last bullet for my girl if need be.'

"'All right, old man,' mumbled Jim. 'I'll see to things, but I still think you ought to stop here and let me take the men up to the drift.'

"'Rot,' answered Tony. 'I've commanded these fellows for three years, and it isn't likely I'd let anyone else take them into action now the time has come; besides, the moral effect would be bad upon the native mind if I let you take on my job. You're a Sapper, Jim, and your place is here.'

"As he made to leave the room I managed to whisper: 'Good-bye, Tony, and the best of luck.' He turned like a flash and came across the room with long, lithe strides.

"'Why, Bruce,' he said, 'this is fine. We've got a bit of a show on. Jim'll tell you all about it. Help him look after the missus.'

"Three days later I was up and about again, but no word had come back from the river and we were beginning to get very anxious. On the fourth morning a native came into the block-house with news that the German troops, having detached a small force to engage Tony's attention, had made a wide detour and crossed the river at a point many miles lower down. They were now almost within striking distance of our post.

"Mrs. Harband never flinched at the news, but I saw her watching Jim in a peculiar way. There was a sort of anxious, almost maternal look in her eyes. Then I looked at him and his big jaw was grimly set. Going to the door he blew his whistle and a bugler came racing across the compound in answer to the summons.

"'Sound the "Alarm,"' said Jim and the clear notes of the bugle rang out upon the instant.

"We manned the outer line of trenches and waited expectantly all day. Next morning we 'stood-to' at dawn. Soon after we saw the first line of German *asikari* creeping over the crest of the hill. They hoped, evidently, to take us by surprise, wherefore we waited for them to get well within range before we loosed off our maxim and rifle fire. Jim had had all the ranges taped and so the execution we did was pretty considerable.

"By noon they had driven us back to our inner line of defences, which left only the barbed wire entanglements and the block-house behind us. In the centre of this section was a large dug-out, to which the wounded and the sick had already been moved.

"It was just as well, for soon after we had taken up our fresh positions a shell pitched right into the compound and made havoc of part of the building, which Mrs. Harband had not yet left. Jim yelled to me to take charge and was out of the trench in an instant. He raced like a madman across the open to the block-house, out of which he reappeared shortly carrying the woman in his arms; blood was streaming down her face and she was unconscious, for a sliver of shell had caught her on the side of the head. The wound was not serious and she was fairly well again when she went off to sit with the wounded in the dug-out an hour later.

"I had seen the look in Jim's eyes when he leaped down into the trench with Tony's wife in his arms and I think that I knew then how things stood with him.

"Towards sunset I was hit twice and had myself carried to the trench where Jim commanded. Things were very bad and the end not far off. Up to the present the Huns had attacked in open order, but that they would attack in mass formation before long there could be no doubt and then our numbers would be up.

"'When they come over the crest in mass,' said Jim, 'I shall fire the mines, and after that it will be a sharp struggle and a quick finish, I fancy.'

"I think it was the concussion when he did fire the mines that brought me back to my senses.

"The five native soldiers and the bugler in our trench were all dead. Mrs. Harband crouched upon the fire-step close to Jim, who was standing up firing grimly and steadily over the parapet. I lay still, watching them, for I didn't feel able to speak; I was too busy keeping my senses from wandering again, for I had been pretty hard hit.

"Suddenly I saw Jim stagger back as a bullet struck him in the right arm, then he shifted the rifle to his left shoulder and went on firing. Presently he slipped to the fire-step and remained leaning against Mrs. Harband.

"'It's all up, Phil,' he whispered; 'they'll charge any time now and that will be the end.'

"'Is there no hope at all?' she asked.

"'None whatever,' he answered, and slipped the revolver from its holster at his side into her hand. 'You are brave enough to do the right thing when the time comes?' he asked.

"'Of course,' she answered. 'But are you sure that there is absolutely no hope?'

"'Not the ghost of a chance now,' he replied.

"'Then it can't matter our telling each other?' she said.

"'Telling what?' he asked.

"'Oh, Jimmie, Jimmie!' she cried, stretching out her hands. 'I know, and it has always been you, my dear.'

"By a superhuman effort he struggled up from the crumpled heap into which he had collapsed and sat staring at her with incredulous eyes.

"'But I don't understand,' he said. 'Do you mean that you love me as I love you?'

"'Yes, yes!' she answered eagerly, 'and always have done. But you never spoke, Jimmy, and then you went away to India and I thought you didn't care; and when Tony came along I was miserable and lonely and so I married him, but it has always been you, really; and when you turned up here six months ago I was frightened for us both, but oh, so dreadfully glad to be near you again. But I would never have told you nor let you suspect even, Jim, if things hadn't turned out like this, for Tony is such a dear and I wouldn't hurt him for the world; but it doesn't matter about our both knowing now, does it?'

"'Of course not and I don't believe old Tony would mind if he knew; but do you mean that you would have married an ugly, empty-headed fool like me if I had asked you?'

"'Yes, my dear,' she answered softly; 'and you're not ugly, only big and strong and rugged, as a man should be.'

"'Hum!' said Jimmie Wardrup; 'it's worth dying to hear you say that first.'

"Then I shut my eyes tightly, for there are some things too sacred to be profaned by the eyes of the onlooker, but I knew that he had gathered her into his arms and that their lips had met in one long kiss.

"Suddenly the firing in front seemed to increase tremendously in volume, then two or three shells of a bigger calibre than had been used before that day went whining overhead, the explosion of which seemed faint. I opened my eyes again. Together Jimmie and I dragged ourselves up to the parapet. Shells were bursting over the German lines and their *asikari* swinging round to face a flank attack.

"It was evident that the relieving forces had arrived and were putting over some shells from in rear of our position. The flank attack was obviously in trouble and likely to be wiped out before the troops accompanying the guns could come to its assistance. In fact, the two attacking forces did not seem to be connected with each other, except by the bond of a common cause.

"'My God! that's old Tony and our own men attacking on the flank!' yelled Jim, and then he seemed to get back all his strength for one final effort. Bending down he snatched up the bugle which had fallen from the fingers of the dead native bugler and, clapping it to his lips, sounded the 'Advance.' With a wild yell he struggled up over the parapet.

"Suddenly I realised that Mrs. Harband was standing beside me as I leaned against the parapet with my weight supported upon my unwounded leg. Her head was fully exposed to the enemy's fire. I tried to force her down into safely, but she shook me off, and together we stood to watch what would happen.

"At the sound of the bugle and Jim's wild yell the native soldiers had popped their heads up over the parapets of their trenches. The sight of him stumbling and lurching forward alone sent them leaping from shelter to join him. Many of them were nearly as badly wounded as their leader, but their discipline was magnificent, the speed of the advance being that of the slowest of the attackers. Many of them dropped, but just before the Bosche lines were reached the remainder raised a cheer and charged in with all the speed and strength they could muster. It was magnificent, but the enemy's ranks had swallowed them in a moment, and after that we did not see them any more.

"Later when we found Jim, he was covered and surrounded by dead men, and so hacked about as to be well-nigh unrecognisable. I fancy the Hun *asikari* had taken their *pangas* to him. But the fury of that final effort had saved the flanking party from annihilation by relieving the pressure just long enough for further help to arrive.

"Tony remained looking down upon his dead comrade for a long time. 'I sometimes think,' he said at last, 'that life didn't treat poor old Jim too well, he was such a grim beggar, but, by God! he has made a great end.'

"I was present when Tony and his wife met. She went straight to his arms and not a tremor of hesitation indicated that the man her soul loved had just laid down his life to save the man who was her husband and for whom she bore only the decorous affection bred of domesticity and close association."

Bruce drew his pipe from his pocket and filled it slowly.

"When you love on that scale, Jack," he said, "you will understand the true meaning of the word, and not until."

VI
THE APE PEOPLE

"I MAINTAIN THAT THE OGRE of folk-lore is not, as so many scientists have held, due to our subconscious recollection of our anthropoid ape ancestors, but rather to a dim racial remembrance of the Neanderthal man who was superseded by the Paleolithic people, the first true men. As Sir Harry Johnstone has told us, the Neanderthalers were 'gorilla-like monsters, with cunning brains, shambling gait, hairy bodies, strong teeth, and possibly cannibalistic tendencies.'

"Another point to be borne in mind is that the great apes are happiest among the trees, whereas man walks and runs with such facility as to indicate a long ancestry upon the ground. It must also be remembered that man walks on his toes and heels, using the great toe as a throw-off, but the three great apes walk on the outer side of the foot, using the middle toe as a lever and never touching the ground with the great toes at all."

With these remarks the eminent anthropologist concluded his address upon the "Explosion of Darwinism," bowed, and left the platform.

Bruce Logan, and his two friends, Hugh Trent and Jack Spenser collected their hats and coats from the attendant, strolled out of the Philharmonic Hall and made their way along Great Portland Street.

Jack Spenser, as was his custom, pulled to pieces the lecture and reconstructed the theory as they walked homewards.

Outside the door of his house in Regent's Terrace, Bruce Logan paused, latch-key in hand.

"If you would care to come in for a smoke and a drink," he said, "I should like to tell you a story brought back to my mind by the lecture to which we have just been listening."

Logan led the way to the study, where whisky, soda-water and sandwiches were set ready upon the sideboard.

"Help yourselves," he said, "and draw the Chesterfield up to the fire. You know where to find the old smoking jacket, Hugh," he added, "and Jack has the cigarettes beside him. Personally, I prefer my old meerschaum pipe and a fill of strong Boer tobacco. Somehow its pungency always seems to bring me back into close touch with the wilds."

"Lucky you aren't married, Bruce," laughed Trent; "your taste in tobacco would drive any woman to desperation."

"Marriage is a double-edged sword which I have no wish to handle," said Bruce. "The poor devil I am going to tell you about tried the experiment unsuccessfully."

"Not one of the eternal triangle problem stories, is it?" asked Spenser.

"Shut up and you will learn!" said Trent, then, turning to his host, he added: "Fire away, Bruce!"

Logan slowly filled and lit his pipe.

"Last time I was in Africa," he commenced, "I was out after leopards for the Zoological Society. That was immediately after the Armistice, when societies all over the world were competing with each other in the race to make good the war shortages.

"I collected my *safari* at Nairobi, went up to Kisumu on the Uganda Railway and crossed Lake Victoria by the 'Clement Hill' to Bukoba, which is in the Karagwe country, where leopards are plentiful. We trekked out along the Kagera River until we got news from the natives of the sort of game I wanted, then we pitched camp and built our traps.

"We had been there about a week and I had already got two very fine leopards, which I hoped to tranship safely to England in due course. They were equivalent to the first hundred and twenty pounds in my pocket.

"Towards dawn one morning I was awakened by the wild, terrible cry of an anthropoid ape. I had neither seen nor heard anything of the big, dangerous brutes in the district and so was rather at a loss to account for that nerve-shattering sound which had awakened me. After awhile it was repeated again, but this time there was a distinct appeal for help in the tones. I waited a long time for the cry to be taken up and answered, but the jungle was still. No answering call rang out.

"I dressed and was having my breakfast, when Buko, my native 'boy,' came running across the clearing in front of my hut with his eyes fairly starting out of his head.

"'*Bwana*,' he cried, 'there is a strange white ape caught in the leopard trap! At least we think it is an ape, for it chatters like one and yet looks half like a man.'

"At this I sprang up and bade him bring my rifle and helmet. I was greatly excited, for I had visions of an entirely new species of anthropoid ape—perhaps the 'missing link'—the discovery of which would most certainly enable me to write the magic letters 'F.Z.S.,' after my name.

"Running swiftly, we soon came to the trap. At the solid wooden bars a most extraordinary apparition was shaking with its hands and tearing with its teeth. I gazed at it in amazement, for, despite the abnormally long arms, hairy body, and heavily-bearded face and long hair, intertwined with leaves and clay, which adorned its head, the creature, as Buko had said, bore a remarkable resemblance to a white man. The sort of white man one imagines as chipping stone implements on the Sussex Downs in the Neolithic Age.

"I spoke to him in English, French, Arabic, and every African native dialect of which I had a knowledge. The effect of all was the same, he merely chattered and occasionally roared like a bull ape.

"After that I sent Buko back to the hut for my medicine chest. I took a big wad of cotton-wool and I saturated it with chloroform. This I put upon the end of a long stick and pushed through the bars of the cage. Instantly the creature fell upon it and began worrying it with his teeth. After a few moments his struggles became less violent, finally he collapsed upon the ground. We raised the door of the cage and bound him securely with ropes, then we carried him back to the camp, where he was put into a hut and covered with blankets.

"That evening when I returned from my day's hunting, Buko told me that the creature, upon awakening, had been very sick and would take no food, but was comparatively quiet.

"I changed my clothes, had my tub, and put on my old Cambridge athletic blazer, which I always wear in the evening when I am out in the wilds.

"After I had had my supper two of the gun-bearers brought in our captive, still securely roped. In the dim light of the two lamps he looked a little less repulsively inhuman, but that effect was perhaps produced only by the two old blankets in which one of the natives had clothed him after their own custom.

"Again I interrogated him in various languages, but with no better success. Presently I noticed that his eyes were fixed intently upon the laurel wreath and lettered 'C.U.A.C.' which adorn the pocket of my blazer. I saw him frame his lips into a semblance of words several times unsuccessfully. At last he said very slowly, 'You Blue.'

"'Yes, yes,' I cried excitedly; 'how do you know?'

"'Me Blue,' he answered instantly.

"After that I tried hard for nearly two hours to get something further out of him, but it was of no use. He was thinking from the back of his brain again and had drifted off into his monkey chatter.

"At last I hit upon a bright notion. I went to my box and unearthed a bunch of picture post-cards and a souvenir book of the Olympic Games. The views of places did not seem to mean anything to him, but the athletic pictures interested him strangely. Finding a picture of a high jumper I placed my finger upon it and said, 'Me.' Then I turned the pages slowly. When we came to the Hammer Throwers, he chattered excitedly for a while, and then burst out, 'Me! me! me!' over and over again.

"You may imagine how puzzled I was. I could get no more out of him, but if I was to believe the little I had learned, it meant that this half-human ape had once been a 'Varsity hammer throwing Blue.

"I kept him with me for a month, and at the end of a week was able to release him from constraint during the daytime; but at night I was bound to tie him up, for, although he had by that time ceased his chattering by day, he always seemed to revert to the ape-type at sunset.

"Human speech didn't come easily to him, but he had already several times said 'Oxford,' 'Blue,' and 'English,' together with the name 'Dick,' which seemed to be ceaselessly recurring in his brain. Every time he said it he looked away towards the forest.

"We had no end of difficulty in feeding him; no cooked food would he touch; but one day, when the boys brought in a buck I had shot, he fell upon it before anyone could prevent him, and tore great lumps of meat with his teeth from the still hot and bleeding carcass.

"It was the most horrible sight I've ever seen. I cuffed him off, but he turned snarling upon me with his teeth bared. Then I spoke to him quietly in English, and instantly he pulled himself together and walked away to his hut.

"At the end of the month he could articulate distinctly with the well-modulated accentuation of the Oxford man, but still he had to speak slowly and, obviously, felt the lack of his former extensive vocabulary. In moments of excitement he still chattered.

"The time was long since past when I should have been back at the coast, but what to do with my strange guest was a problem which was beginning seriously to exercise my mind. However, the matter was settled without my having to come to a decision, as you will see.

"One evening, long after Norton—as I will call him, although that was not his name—had discarded his dirty red blankets for one of my suits, we were sitting in my *banda* after supper, which, in common with other meals, we now shared. Suddenly he turned to me, after a long silence in which I had filled and lit my pipe.

"'Logan,' he said, in the slow, methodical manner he had acquired, 'you do not know my name, but maybe you will collect evidence and piece it together when you return and so perhaps something of my story will reach the ears of some member of my family, which is an old and noble one. I would rather tell you the tale myself if you will promise not to abuse my confidence by seeking out my true identity.'

"I gave him the required assurance, and then he told me what must surely be one of the strangest stories in the world. I will tell it to you as far as possible in his own words.

"'Even as a child,' he commenced, 'I had no playmates, for other children feared my ugliness. At school it was the same. I was nicknamed the "Baboon" on account of my bow-legs, deep chest and long arms. At Oxford, whither I went in due season, my great strength and agility gained me a certain degree of popularity in athletic circles, for I could throw the hammer as no man had ever thrown it before. I outclassed all my opponents at the Inter-University sports, and in the same year won the English championship.

"'People said I was certain to establish a new world's record, for I had brains as well as brute force at my command. Doubtless I should have done so but for an unfortunate incident which altered the whole course of my life. A freakish whim had led me to accentuate my ape-like ugliness by letting my hair grow until that of my head came down to my eye-brows and met my whiskers growing up from below.

"'One evening when I was returning with some friends from the Bullingdon, where we had been spending the evening, we came upon a cabby holding his horse up short by the head and beating it unmercifully with the stock of his whip.

"'Hastening across the road, I laid my hand upon the man's shoulder and begged him to desist. He turned quickly upon me.

"'"Why you — monkey," he said, "for two pins I'd take my whip to you."

"'The reference to my personal appearance, combined with his treatment of the horse, so enraged me that I quite lost control of my temper. Snatching the whip from his hands I beat him until it splintered into a hundred fragments. I then heaved him high above my head and dashed him down upon the cobbled paving of the Corn Market.

"'Then my rage left me and I became aware of a battered form lying at my feet, from the lips and nostrils of which black blood oozed stickily.

"'My companions drew back from me in horrified alarm and I walked back to college alone. But first I called a cab in which the injured man was removed to hospital.

"'Next morning I was arrested and, needless to say, I was subsequently sent down. Great publicity was given to the case; this so enraged my father that he gave me a thousand pounds and bade me go overseas and stop there.

"'A week later I sailed for Africa. On the boat I met a girl whose brother had been one of my few intimate friends up at Oxford. Curiously enough, neither my personal appearance nor past record seemed to repel her, as I had expected would be the case. Her pet fetishes apparently were strength and courage, which were probably my two sole redeeming qualities.

"'We were continually together throughout the long voyage and, at Cape Town, we were married.

"'We sailed on up the coast to Mombassa and traveled inland to Nairobi, which at that time was no more than a small frontier post, for the Government had not then moved inland from the coast.

"'I took up land and started farming with what remained of my thousand pounds. From the very beginning things went well. We lived in grass huts at first, but soon built a decent wooden bungalow, and then the crops were cultivated and the stock we raised began to show handsome returns. Only one thing was lacking to make our happiness complete and that, too, was given to us in due course, when our little son Dick was born.

"'I sent my wife and child home for a year, as I could well afford to do. When they came back Irene was changed, nothing tangible that one could take hold of, but the simple life of the wilds didn't seem to content her any more. She was moody and silent for whole days together.

"'About that time the amateur big-game hunters—"slaugh-terers" they should be called—were beginning to find out the pos-sibilities of East Africa. One day a typical specimen of the tribe turned up at our *shamba*. You never saw such a kit in all your life as he had brought with him. Tinned goods enough to stock a colony, guns to fit out a battalion pretty well and patent camp equipment galore and, of course, he'd brought a professional hunter to see that he didn't come to harm and to shoot all the dangerous game for him.

"'I was glad enough of his coming at first; for association with someone fresh out from England seemed to cheer Irene up. God! What a blind fool I was!

"'He seemed quite content to make his hunting headquarters at my place. After he'd been with us a month I had to go on a ten days' *safari* to pick up a mob of cattle from a wandering Somali who was coming down from Uganda. At Ford's suggestion I took his professional hunter, Harris, with me for company.

"'We came back in just over three weeks, but I knew that some-thing was wrong the moment I came in sight of the house. There was an uncared-for look about everything, and all the "boys" were idle.

"'I ran up the verandah steps and into the bungalow. The whole place was inches thick in dust. Harris stood outside the door whis-tling through his teeth and looking mighty uncomfortable. I shouted for my personal "boy," who came running in double quick time.

"'I asked him where my wife was.

"'"The *bibi* has gone away with the white Bwana," he told me.

"'"When?" I asked him.

"'"Oh, soon after you went on safari," he answered.

"'"Where was my son?" I asked next.

"'"They had taken the *toto* with them," he said.

"'I searched the place. There was no letter, no message, only the information the black boy could give me. I seized Harris and shook him by the shoulder, asking what it meant.

"'"Easy enough to see," he said. "They've cleared. We'd best be getting down to the coast after them."

"'Three days' *safari* from my *shamba* we came upon an old camp. Close to the scattered ashes of a fire we found the skeletons of a man and a woman picked clean by the jackals and the white ants. There was no doubt whose they were, for the little silver crucifix which my wife had always worn and which no native would willingly touch, for they held it to be powerful "medicine," was still suspended by its chain round the neck of the female skeleton.

"'It was easy enough to see what had happened. That fool Ford, who knew not one word of Swahili, had got at logger-heads with his own natives and they had finished him and Irene too. But there was no sign of a child's bones. Of course, a wandering beast might have carried off my little Dick and devoured him in its lair, but somehow I did not feel as if he was dead.

"'Harris wanted me to go on down to the coast with him, but I would not do so, for I felt that I must stay and look for Dick. I couldn't bear to live in our old home, so I burned it down and let the fields lie fallow. I wandered all over the country, from tribe to tribe and village to village seeking news everywhere, but without result.

"'After about three years of this life, I gave up hope and went straight through to Uganda elephant hunting. There was no job too risky for me to take on. I wanted to die. I've stood up to wounded beasts with only one cartridge in my rifle time and again and I've killed leopards, Nandi fashion, with a red blanket round one arm and a shortened spear in the hand of the other. But the more risks I took the less harm came to me. The more careless I was of my health the stronger I grew. At last I discarded firearms altogether and went to live with the Masai. From them I went to the Wanderobo, the forest tree-dwellers, who are just about as low in the scale of humanity as any people well can be. With them I roamed the country from end to end, but after awhile I left them and wandered alone. I never spoke to a soul, until I well-nigh lost the power of speech and was nothing better than a skin-clad savage living by my spear and bow. Time had lost all significance for me and, always, I avoided the haunts of men.

"'After many wanderings I came to a part of the country which seemed to be absolutely uninhabited except by wild beasts and the big anthropoid apes, whose habits I studied covertly.

"'One day I saw what appeared to be a white ape go swinging through the middle terrace of the trees, and something stirred within me. I was feeling emotion again after many years.

"'I followed that particular tribe of apes for what was probably many weeks. Then, just before dawn one morning, as I lay in the shelter I had built for myself, I heard a terrific struggle close at hand. I crept quietly out on hands and knees, and there I saw a white man forcing a big Oryx buck to the ground and tearing at its throat with his teeth.

"'The youth would have been about seventeen years of age, and I knew him at once. Despite his bronze, he was wonderfully like my dead wife, and about his neck hung a locket which we had placed there when he was a year old.

"'Stripping off my scanty clothing, so that I might look as much like him as possible, and dropping my weapons, I stepped out into the clearing with my hands extended. Instantly he left the Oryx bull and flew at me; but, strong as he was, I bore him down and held him. Then he sent forth the call of the apes, which turned the blood cold in my veins, but still I hung on.

"'Down from the trees dropped the great hairy brutes and, in a moment, I was torn from my hold. I called to my son, but he appeared not to understand me. Then they carried me away, deeper into the forest than I had ever penetrated before. They did not harm me, why I do not know, unless it was on account of some likeness I may have borne to my son, who appeared to be their leader.

"'That night he came to me. I stretched out my hand and touched the locket about his neck. He took it off and held it out to me. Taking it in my hand I touched the spring when, to his evident amazement it flew open. I showed him the photograph of myself beside that of his mother. He looked from it to me many times and at last seemed to understand.

"'From that time onwards I have lived the life of an ape of the tribe under my own son's leadership. I have never taught him to speak any human language, for I believe that we are happier as we are. But he has taught me the brief vocabulary of the apes, so that we are able to talk together a little.

"'When I fell into your trap I was hunting alone in this place; when you let me go I shall forget all about civilisation again and shall go back to my own people.'"

* * * * * * *

Logan paused for some moments after this long narration.

"You can see," he said at last, "how difficult it was for me to determine what was my duty in the peculiar circumstances.

"That night," he continued, "I heard the call of the ape-people twice repeated, but thought only that it was my guest venting his feelings. In the morning we found the hut in which he had slept torn all to pieces. There were the tracks of big apes all around the place, and mingled with them were the imprints of two distinct sets of human feet."

Logan leaned forward and carefully scraped out the bowl of his pipe.

"It was the best thing that could have happened in the circumstances," he said.

"Yes," said Jack Spenser, "but one begins to wonder if there is not something in this theory of Darwin's after all."

VII
THE SOUL OF A NATIVE

THERE WERE TWO SOUTH AFRICAN SOLDIERS, an ex-officer of the King's African Rifles, and a commercial traveler, all trying to make the best of a meagre fire the porter had kindled in the waiting-room stove before going off duty for the night.

The four had inadvertently entered a slip-carriage at Waterloo, and were now, therefore, doomed to a four hours' wait at this wayside station, whereas they had anticipated the comfort of beds at Southampton.

They had talked for a while, and then had tried to sleep; but, old campaigners though three of them were, they found the cold, away from the small radius of the fire's warmth, well-nigh unbearable; their blood had been thinned by over-long sojourning under tropical skies. The commercial traveler, upon the other hand, did not seem unduly bothered by the bitter night, but found it impossible to compose his limbs to the hardness of the bench upon which he had sought sleep.

"I see from your belongings that all you gentlemen have seen service during the war," he said. "Personally I was rejected, which was perhaps as well, since I'm sure I could never have stood the hardships—although, mark you, I'd have done my best. But I've been used to dry underclothing and a good bed all my life; it beats me how ever you managed to sleep in those terrible damp trenches."

"Damp did you say?" asked one of the South Africans. "My bloomin' oath, I should just about say they was damp."

88

"Yes, but we didn't mind that," interposed his comrade. "It was the bitter cold which caused us to suffer so terribly."

"Ah!" said the first speaker, Piet Schwartz. "This ain't no country for the likes of us. Give me the big, open back veldt, and damn the niggers, says I."

"Niggers!" exclaimed John Leys, who had attained commissioned rank in the South African Infantry, "Niggers! I hate the whole damn lot of them."

"They must indeed be a great trial to you people who live in the wilds," said the commercial traveler interestedly. "I understand that they are little better than animals, and treacherous to a degree?"

"True for you," answered Schwartz. "Animals they are, and like animals you have to manage them—if you don't want your throat cut or your food poisoned. They haven't any brains, feelings nor affections."

"There you are entirely wrong," said Captain Hamlyn, the K.A.R. officer, who had not hitherto spoken. "You can hardly say that such men as T'Chaka or Cetewayo, of the Amazulu, were without brains, and I think I could prove conclusively to you that the East African native, at all events, is faithful and capable of the most lasting affection. We have a saying in the King's African Rifles that the *asikari*—that is native soldiers—will never leave their officers, either 'dead, damned or done for.' They gave a fine example of this at Namacurru on the Quilimane River. A battalion of the 3rd K.A.R. was trapped by the Germans and the men sacrificed their lives in hundreds to give their comrades time to recover the body of a favourite officer."

"Yes, I've heard that many of the East African tribesmen make good soldiers," said Leys; "but I think Schwartz had in mind personal affection, as between man and woman, when he spoke. Isn't that so, Piet?"

"That's right," responded the Afrikander.

"Generally speaking," said Hamlyn, "the East African native bases his sex relations upon Rudyard Kipling's axiom, of which he has, of course, never heard, that 'woman is made by a blind

Providence for one purpose, and one purpose only.' The native who thinks otherwise is a variation from the normal.

"It may also be accepted as true that ninety-nine per cent. of African native women are repulsively ugly, when judged from our Western standpoint, but have beautiful figures.

"The native woman who is blessed—or cursed—with regular, aquiline and pleasing features is also a departure from the normal.

"When two such anomalies meet and mate there is, not infrequently, considerable trouble."

"It sounds as if there might be a story behind those remarks," said Leys, with a knowing smile.

"Not exactly a story," answered Hamlyn, "but certain sets of circumstances which go far to justify my contention that the black man is, on the whole, a good fellow; but one whose ways are incomprehensible to us, since his whole scheme of existence is governed by different standards. Western peoples regard the African savage as primitive, but, in reality, he has reached the highest pitch of evolution, according to his own lights; and, for him, all the problems of life were settled untold generations ago. You must remember that the ethnologists hold that the African people have probably lived just as they are living to-day for at least a hundred thousand years."

There was a long pause before the commercial traveler, who had been much impressed, summoned up the courage to speak.

"All my life," he said, "I've had a terrible desire to see the world, but in that matter I haven't been as lucky as you gentlemen. I'd take it as a great favour, sir," he added, speaking directly to Hamlyn, "if you'd tell us something about your experiences out there."

"Yes," interposed Leys; "we've nearly four hours to wile away in this dreary hole. Won't you give us the tale of your two anomalies?"

Hamlyn slowly filled his pipe, staring reminiscently into the fire-glow as he assembled the recollections of other years. When his pipe was drawing to his satisfaction he settled himself a little more comfortably into the angle of the wall, against which the bench was pushed.

"If you had lived along the German East African border any time prior to August, 1914," he said, "you would have had an excellent chance of seeing and hearing things which would have made you wonder why the world had waxed so angry over the Belgian atrocities in the Congo, and yet raised no protest at the activities of the white officers and N.C.O.s employed in German East Africa.

"The Bosche was naturally beastly-minded, as the world quickly discovered when he established himself in Flanders in 1914. We were aware of his ways long before that. There were rumours—nasty, ugly tales, told by the natives, which would have made any decent white man's blood run cold.

"Apparently the ancient Spanish edition of the feudal system appealed to them. In consequence if a Bosche officer, or N.C.O. for that matter, saw a woman who found favour in his eyes he simply told the native sergeant-major to see that she was sent to his quarters and it did not matter two hoots in hell either if the woman was a *binti* or a *bibi*—that is to say, a maiden or a wife—for the Hun had rather less morals than the natives he affected so deeply to despise.

"The post I commanded in 1913 was smack on the edge of the German border. It was marked 'dangerous' on the secret maps at headquarters and I knew full well how likely it was to produce a big batch of difficulties at any moment.

"In the first place, we had never properly conquered the natives in that district and they were none too friendly, either to us or the Bosche, so that we might find ourselves allied with the German troops against the *shenzis*—that is, 'wild natives'—any day. But in the backs of our British minds there was always the suspicion that it was against the Germans themselves that we should see service soonest.

"Anyway, the general situation served to keep me vigilant, and I had a pretty thorough secret service of my own at work before I had been at M'Blano six months. In consequence, there was very little that went on, either side of the border, that did not come to my knowledge sooner or later, usually sooner.

"The head of my 'secret police' was a Lamu man of very light colour, called Kombo bin M'Bwana. He was blessed with the keen intellect of his Persian forefathers.

"One morning early he entered my *banda* and, standing stiffly to attention, awaited permission to speak.

"'*Habari gani?*' said I, giving the conventional Swahili greeting, which also asks for news.

"To which he replied, '*Ote mzuri*,' which means that 'All is well,' and then, as is also the native's custom, he commenced to set out all that was wrong.

"After a long recital of many small happenings of minor interest, he paused, assembling his thoughts, as it were, before delivering his peroration.

"'*Effendi*,' he said, 'there are a man and woman who dwell in the forest, being of no village and of no tribe known to me, but the man is tall and very strong; it is said that last moon he slew with his naked hands a leopard which attacked the woman, he has a shining ring of black wood, or perhaps gum, worked into his hair. They live in two huts, each shaped like the half of a ball and having a small opening through which one must enter upon all fours.

"'The man's name is Umbelazi, and the woman he calls Nava. He, who is sparing of speech, silent even in appearance, and terrible in dispute, as some of the young men of the villages know full well, treats not the woman as is our custom, but as an equal. When they walk abroad she does not follow him, but walks at his side, holding long converse, but when at the huts it is said that he helps even with her duties.'

"'What say they of them in the villages?' I asked.

"'That they hold themselves outside the village laws, but break none,' came the answer.

"I made further inquiries, through such sources as are known to those who hold authority in savage countries; but, receiving no bad report, left the couple to their own devices, making myself a mental promise, however, to take a look at them at the first opportunity which offered.

"One day they vanished.

"The bush, impenetrable, unknown, absorbed them; nor could the most diligent inquiry through the villages elicit any information concerning them.

"No one had seen them go. The huts were left untouched, the cooking pots were in place, the crop of maize they had cultivated grew to ripeness in the garden, but no weapons had been left behind—a significant fact, when considered in conjunction with the presence of the cooking utensils, without which no native undertakes a long journey. And because they had sojourned in my district and were, therefore, of my people, I wanted to know more about this strange and sudden exodus. There was, however, little that I could do beyond sending orders to my intelligence men to be on the look-out for the missing strangers; and, anyway, the most mysterious happenings are apt to have the most natural explanations—in Africa.

"About that time a Border Commission was due, to investigate certain points in dispute between ourselves and the Germans; and, having received orders to collect information to lay before them, I assembled a small *safari* and set out along the frontier.

"Some thirty miles away from M'Blano a German post was located at Kionga, and thither I made my way.

"Ten miles short of Kionga I came to a sudden halt, hearing shouts of laughter ahead, followed by a piercing scream in a woman's voice. The laughter was obviously European, since the white man laughs 'Ha! Ha! Ha!' and the native 'Ho! Ho! Ho!'

"Going cautiously forward, I parted the screen of leaves and looked out upon the clearing beyond.

"Roped to a tree was a big native of stern countenance and imposing proportions. His muscles stood out in knotty bunches beneath the glistening black skin as he strained against the constricting ropes. In the centre of the clearing a woman, who had been flung face downwards, writhed under the hands of four German *asikari*; a fifth stood over her holding in his hand a heavy *kiboko*, as we call the hippopotamus-hide whip which in South

Africa is known as a *sjambok*. In a camp chair, set well back in the shade, lolled a fat Bosche, who laughed uproariously at the struggles of his victims.

"No more than a glance was needed to show me that the woman was almost at her last gasp. The flesh of her back was cut to ribbons. The convulsive twitching of her limbs grew less spasmodic as I watched.

"Shouting an order to the *asikari* who wielded the *kiboko* to stand back, I sprang into the clearing. At the same moment the big Bosche heaved himself up from his deck chair and ran heavily forward. There was a furious, almost insane, light in his eyes, and his fingers were fumbling at the fastenings of his revolver holster as he advanced. His jaw was thrust forward most invitingly, and I let him have it, too—as nice and clean an uppercut as you could wish to see.

"Having put the Hun to sleep, I turned my attention to the woman. As I have said, her body was pretty badly lacerated and there was a hard swelling, of a most peculiar nature, in the left armpit; but she was not beyond aid. I had a native medical orderly with me, whom I bade wash and dress her wounds.

"While I had been making the examination and giving my orders, Kombo bin M'Bwana had released the big native from his bonds. As I turned he leaped to his feet, with hand held high above his head, palm outwards, in salute, and the word he uttered in a deep, resonant voice was '*Inkoos.*'

"Word and gesture were alike familiar, but it was the ring of black gum worked into the hair and lightly polished with fat which assembled old memories and told me that he was of the Zulu people.

"You are of the children of Cetewayo?' I asked.

"'You speak truth, *Inkoos*,' he said. 'My daughter and I are both of the Amazulu and have traveled far, to an evil place it seems, where some white men are no better than the *Amaboma* (Boers).'

"His words somehow bore the stamp of truth, and yet it seemed well-nigh incredible that these two should have traveled safely more than four thousand miles and through a hundred hostile peoples. Yet there could be no doubt that he was a *keshla*—a ringed man—who had probably seen service in Cetewayo's *impis*. These things I knew from the moment he raised his hand in salute and addressed me as 'Chief.'

"I might have questioned him further, but the Bosche came to his senses and sent a bullet whistling past my ear. In a flash the big Zulu was upon him, pinning him down.

"'Stand off!' I shouted. 'Do you not know the custom that no black man shall lay hands upon the white?'

"To the Bosche I said: 'I cannot arrest you, for we are upon German territory, where your authority runs; but I shall report this through my Government to yours and I hope you will get your deserts.'

"'English swine,' he answered. 'My Government will know how to deal with you Gott-damt people,' and at that we left it.

"That night I made camp my own side of the border. As I sat at my tent door after supper the big Zulu came to me and, having been given permission, squatted down upon his heels to tell his story.

"'Baba,' he said, addressing me now as 'Father,' which is a mark of supreme confidence among the Zulu people, 'we have wandered far to your land, bearing the secret that is sacred and the treasure that is hidden; for the *Amaboma* knew of the treasure and would have taken it from us. Here we knew that the English, who are just, held sway, wherefore we wished to dwell as dogs in the shadow of your hut.'

"'Why, then, did you go away?' I asked.

"'Baba, we did not go away,' he answered. 'But coming through the country of the white people called *Germani*, he whom you struck to-day saw my daughter, Nava, and desiring her for himself, set his spies to watch us. One day, when I was away hunting, his soldiers came secretly to the hut and bore her off. When I returned and found her gone I waited not, but, taking only my battle-axe, followed quickly upon their tracks.

"'At Kionga the battle fury came upon me and I slew men, but others overpowered me. They bound me to a tree, and would have tortured Nava before my eyes, to punish me for my presumption and because she would not bow to the white man's will.'

"'Grow great in my shadow,' I answered. 'The *indaba* is finished.' And with that he went off. Next day we reached my headquarters at M'Blano.

"The woman, Nava, did not recover as quickly as I had expected. Two mornings later, at about 3 o'clock, I heard the sentry challenge and then Umbelazi's voice outside the *banda*. He seemed to think that his daughter was dying and asked me to come to her.

"She was certainly very bad when I reached the hut. There was a nasty grey look beneath the black flesh which I did not at all like. It was not her lacerated back alone that was troubling her, but spasmodic pains in the stomach, which doubled her up every other second.

"For four-and-twenty hours I never left her. I tried hot flannels, brandy, rubbing, and other homely remedies such as one uses in the wilds, but without effect. At last I had recourse to chlorodyne, increasing the doses to dangerous proportions as she seemed to grow worse. And all the while old Umbelazi squatted on his heels at the head of the bed, rocking himself to and fro in an agony of apprehension.

"Only once did he speak and that when I touched the swelling beneath his daughter's arm. I thought it might be the cause of her illness, but he became greatly agitated, and begged of me that I would neither touch nor look at the lump.

"For some while before the dawn she lay still, unconvulsed, but apparently in extremis. I could do no more. Then, just as the first grey streaks of daylight were stealing in through the thin grass walls, she turned her head, so that her cheek lay against my hand.

"'Go to your rest now, *Baba*,' she said; 'the daylight comes, and with it shall I find new life.' And even as she said, so it was.

"Shortly after this a draft of recruits arrived from headquarters, and amongst them a tremendous young Nubian, named Doka Fademula. He and Umbelazi were both jet black and, I think, the finest pair of warriors I have ever seen. But I remember the old Zulu, who evinced a great liking for the Nubian, saying to him upon one occasion, when he was helping him to get ready his khaki kit for parade: 'Ah! it is very fine, but you would have looked more a man behind a buffalo-hide shield and with the white tails beneath your knees.'

"Umbelazi was not, however, the only one who conceived a fondness for the big Nubian. Nava also cast eyes of affection upon him. He was not slow in responding. But that wooing went not according to the way of the native. Rather was it upon the lines of a European courtship, in that he plucked for her great bunches of white lilies and paid her other tributes of civilised affection.

"Then he built a hut and they set up house together, according to tribal custom; but still he remained the lover, treating her always as an equal rather than as a legalised servant.

"Their happiness was, alas, short-lived, and at last he reverted to his savage state.

"News reached me that the Wanyamwezi had risen and were harrying the river villages. Gathering my forces, I set out to check their depredations, leaving only a small guard to hold the station, and in that guard was Doka, the Nubian. Umbelazi went with me.

"There was not a man left alive to tell what had happened when I returned to M'Blano from a fruitless pursuit upon a false report. But the tale was all too plain to read. The guard had died fighting to the last man: the women and children had been carried off. Before his hut Doka Fademula lay dead, his head crushed in and all his wounds in front. He had discarded his khaki kit and rifle in favour of old Umbelazi's war finery and battle-axe. With it he had done terrible execution. Of Nava there was no sign.

"'This is a bad *shauri*,' said I, turning to my sergeant-major, Kombo bin M'Bwana, who stood at my elbow. 'Whose is the work?'

"'It is the work of well-trained soldiers, *Effendi*,' he answered, 'for their dead show how regularly they have advanced against the position held by the guard; and yet among their dead are men of many tribes. This is a hard business to understand.'

"I thought things over for a while, but could find no light. Then I asked for Umbelazi. It seemed strange to me that the father of Nava should be absent at that moment.

"'Effendi' said Kombo, 'the Induna'—for so we had come to call the old warrior, who in his day had commanded one of Cetewayo's *impis*—'the Induna sat late by the fire last night with one who cast

the bones and foretold strange things. This morning at daylight he
had gone.'

"'Why did you not report this to me?' I asked sharply.

"'The Induna was not of the command, *Effendi*,' answered the
bashouish. I said no more, for his words were true.

"Having set my *asikari* to work straightening things up, I went
inside the hut Doka had built, and there I found a dead spearman
of the attacking forces and two women, dead also. From the wounds
upon their bodies and the bloody hatchet, still clasped in the dead
hand of one of them, it was evident that they, too, had put up a
grim fight to a finish. As it subsequently transpired, they had died
in a vain attempt to save Nava from capture. And this Umbelazi
told me later—it is significant, too—that wherever Nava went men,
and women, too, were willing to die in her defence, not because of
her beauty only—and she was far more beautiful than a native has
any business to be, but because of a something of which I did not
then know.

"Messages were sent to headquarters, asking that the German
officer commanding at Kionga might be interrogated. My spies
went out in every direction, but the only unusual information they
brought in tended to indicate that all the known bad characters
and many others who were under suspicion, were leaving the district. We could get no tidings of Nava, nor Umbelazi, nor any word
of the force that had been abroad the night before I returned to
M'Blano.

"Every night, as I lay awake beneath my mosquito netting, long
after the noises of the camp had died down and given place to the
night sounds of predatory bush beasts, I had the impression of a
person near me, trying to tell me something; but, apparently, I was
unresponsive to the influence.

"Then came a night of the most awful storm. The thunder
crashed like the clanging of the Gates of Doom. The heavens opened
and shut and the lightning ran about the sky in streams of lam-
bent fire. But no rain fell from the sullen, coppery clouds.

"Never before nor since have I witnessed such an absolute par-
oxysm of Nature; the whole world seemed to await the climax. At

midnight it came. A few drops of rain fell, hissing upon the hot earth. Suddenly the heavens split asunder. In the sustained light I saw the figure of a native woman, clad in naught but a *moocha*, walking towards me from the edge of the bush.

"She halted within a pace of me and I saw that the woman was Nava. Her left arm and shoulder were swathed in tightly-bound wrappings.

"'Greetings, *Inkoos*,' she said, as she raised her right hand.

"'Greeting, Nava,' I answered. 'Whence come you, and why?'

"'I come bearing tidings,' she answered. 'Three days after you set out to seek the Wanyamwezi, who, you were told, had risen, the *Germani* lord sent his soldiers, disguised, to take me. The fight was long and fierce, and at the last Doka slew many before the hut, wherein I waited with two companions. When our enemies had slain Doka they broke into the hut, and then two women who were with me leaped up and fought to the last in my defence.

"'I was borne away to Kionga, but no harm befell me, for the people had learned of the treasure I bore hidden and would not let the white lord work his will. But he kept me prisoner, in the hope, I think, that he would be moved to another place, where he would take me among strange people who would know naught of my history, of which he, too, was ignorant, although he knew that I was not as other natives.'

"She paused for a moment, with head inclined as if to catch the words of a voice speaking from the heart of the storm to her alone.

"'Three days ago,' she continued 'word came to me that big war is brewing and that soon the *Germani* soldiers will come to this and other of the British posts to make an end.'

"At that I caught her up sharply, asking if she was quite certain of her information.

"'Quite, quite certain, *Baba*,' she answered; then turning, pointed to the lightning, which flashed and writhed like a hundred fiery serpents. 'See,' she said, 'where the *Inkoos-i-zana-y-Zulu*—the Mother of the Heavens—rides the sky, a harbinger of strife.'

"Presently all her tale seemed to be finished, and 'Why do you not ask for your father, Umbelazi?' I said.

"'*Baba*,' she replied, 'we have dwelt in your shadow, as you promised, receiving life and many other favours at your hands. My father even now is about your business, as I, too, have been.'

"'What do you mean?' I queried. 'Tell me more.'

"'*Baba*,' she said again patiently, 'you know us only as poor wanderers; you know naught of our greatness, except that Umbelazi was once an Induna of that Great, Great One, the Black Elephant, whose tread shook all the earth before his might melted and he passed to his rest. But you know not that Umbelazi was chief Induna and first counselor to the Lion of Zulu, whose name I may not mention, since he is dead.'

"'And you?' I asked. 'Who are you, Nava, and what secret do you hold, what treasure do you carry?'

"'I am the descendant of that Great, Great One who is gone, holder of the Hereditary Chieftainship, seed sprung from Senzangecona's loins. Watcher of the Resting place of the Kings of Amazulu, Bearer of the Sacred Insignia of the Kings, the great diamond which the *Inkoos-i-zana-y-Zulu* cast down from the heavens when our nation came to birth.'

"For a while she fell silent, nor could I find any words to say, for I was lost in amazement. Then she continued speaking, as one who repeats words put into her mouth.

"'To save the treasure,' she said, 'we left Zululand, for the *Amaboma* had found out the whereabouts of the jewel and would have taken it. Yet, at the last, it has gone from me but my snake tells me that it will be recovered and returned to safe keeping at the Resting Place of the Kings.'

"'How have you lost it?' I asked. 'Has the *Germani* taken it from you?'

"'The *Germani* has it, but I gave it to him. When I heard that your life was threatened I talked with my snake and made a little bargain, my life for yours—you who have been so good to us—if with the sacred jewel I might buy my freedom to come and warn you. After that I cut out the diamond from beneath my armpit and— I am here!'

"'It shall be regained,' I said.

"'Tell Umbelazi,' she said proudly, "that he shall stand by my throne in the heavens, he who has been as a father to me upon earth, although he is not of the Blood Royal.'

"Suddenly she turned her back upon me, throwing wide her arms and gazing upwards to the sky.

"'The hour of payment has come,' she cried. 'See where the *Inkoos-i-zana* rides down the heavens to give me welcome.'

"There was a blinding flash of lightning, which sent me staggering back, with my arm flung up to protect my eyes; a shattering, rending crash of thunder, and then abysmal silence.

"The storm was completely ended.

"When a lantern was brought its light revealed the charred corpse of Nava.

"All through the rest of that night we laboured to perfect our defences, for there was no doubt in my mind that Nava had spoken true words.

"At dawn a brother officer arrived, with orders that I should hand over the command to him and report at headquarters as speedily as possible.

"Two hours later I was on my way down country.

"After four hours' marching I reached the first river, only to find it in flood and the ford impassable. Soon I caught the faint echo of a mutter of firing far away. Shortly after a runner came panting to the riverbank, who wrung his hands to find the water a roaring torrent, which barred his way. Turning, he saw me and sprang to the salute.

"'*Effendi*,' said he, 'I go to headquarters for help. The *Germani asikari* attack us in great numbers and not long may the post be held, unless help is found.'

"There was nothing I could do to aid him and yet I had almost made up my mind to turn back and lend a hand, when suddenly I caught the sound of many feet running swiftly.

"I drew my revolver and waited.

"Presently there emerged into the open, from a forest path, fully four hundred warriors, armed variously, and with old Umbelazi at their head. He was clad in all the splendid panoply of war, proper

to the dignity of a Zulu *induna*. Swiftly the warriors wheeled, forming into four ranks, with Umbelazi in the forefront of the centre.
For a moment they stood like black graven images. Then up shot
his right hand, grasping a battle-axe and up shot the right hands
of all his followers, as the royal salute *'Koom'* boomed out on a
deep resonant note.

"'What is the meaning of this, Umbelazi?' I asked.

"'*Inkoos*,' he answered, 'more than a moon ago I had word that ere
long the hyenas would feed full, then went I away and gathered these
nameless ones, who would retrieve their honour, if that be your will.'

"'What would you do?' I asked.

"'We would fight for that Great, Great White One who sits
across the Black Water,' came the instant response.

"'So be it,' I said. 'We will go back to M'Blano.'

"Then followed one of the most amazing races in the history of
the world, a race against time to save the British frontier.

"At first we moved along at a steady trot and in silence, but
after half a mile had been traversed the pace increased, The rhythm
of the run seemed to have stolen into the men's blood, awakening
all their latent savagery. They began to sing a wonderful song. Just
one man would shout a phrase in high-pitched, long-drawn notes,
then the whole lot roared back the response in deep, booming
tones. My God! it was amazing. One felt the power of it firing one's
own blood. All thought of the stress of sustained effort was forgotten. The rhythm changed, and now everyone was singing. Here and
there a man lifted up his hands and shook his weapons and shield.
Here and there a man leaped high into the air as he shouted fiercely
and between whiles they stamped their feet altogether as they ran.
There was a peculiarly dead, stale smell in the air and yet, somehow, I did not mind it, for the wonder of watching the supple
muscles rippling beneath black skins, glistening with sweat, had
gripped my imagination. By the time we came to the gorge where
we had to climb slowly and carefully down broken rocks the blood
was drumming in my ears, and my breath was coming in great sobbing gasps, so that I was grateful for the break in the rhythm of
movement. And now we caught the sound of firing nearer and more

distinct. Up the other side of the gorge we climbed and soon were running hard again, still singing. Once I fell and for a brief instant heard the wild rush of feet padding past me; but I was up again, almost as my body touched the ground, and in a couple of minutes had regained my place in the van.

"M'Blano was very near now. Only another quarter of a mile, I told myself, and we should see the fight raging below. Only another two hundred yards, but my eyes were almost blind, and I think I'd have given my soul to stop and lie down; but I felt that the natives were watching me keenly. I managed to shout a coarse joke in Swahili and got a roar of laughter in response.

"Someone thrust the rhinoceros horn haft of an axe into my hand; and at the feel of it every symptom of exhaustion vanished. I was seeing red for the first time in my life.

"Through the shattered ranks of our comrades we raged, still singing, and then—my God!—then we were into the Bosche and the singing ceased.

"On every hand I heard the laboured grunt of men who fought fiercely and in silence; the long-drawn, choking groans of the dying and, ever at my side, the savage 'S'gee! S'gee!' with which old Umbelazi despatched his foes.

"Suddenly I found myself face to face with the German officer who had commanded at Kionga. At the sight of me he threw up his hands, but I was a savage then. I sent in a crashing blow and saw the half-moon blade of the axe bite deep into his neck, just at the junction of the body.

"Then the madness left me. But I remembered all that Nava had said. I searched the dead Hun's pockets and found the most amazing diamond concealed in one of them.

"I took the jewel and, finding the battle over, went in search of Umbelazi. I feared that I should not find him, for one does not expect even a seasoned warrior of more than sixty summers to run such a race as we had run and to come unscathed at the end of it through such a fight as we had fought.

"At length I saw him. He was standing in the midst of a ring of dead men, leaning wearily upon the haft of his bloody battle-axe.

He raised the weapon above his head in salute as he caught sight of me.

"'*Wa Inkoos!*' he exclaimed with a grim, delighted chuckle. 'That was a fight worth living for!"

"Then he caught sight of the great diamond where it sparkled upon the palm of my extended hand. A low exclamation burst from his lips, and every sign of tiredness seemed to leave him as his eyes fastened themselves upon the precious stone. He fell upon his knees and bowed his grizzled head in the dust; and many others among the natives did likewise.

"'*Inkoos*,' he said, as he took the stone from my hand, 'give me permission to depart to-morrow, for now I know that my days are numbered and I would journey far to lay the Star of the Heavens in safe keeping at the Resting Place of Kings, before I go to render an account of my stewardship to that Great, Great One, whose tread once shook the earth and at whose word whole nations fell flat."

"'*Hamba gahle!* Go in peace!' I answered in the Zulu tongue and at my word his right hand shot up in salute as the royal 'Bayete' rolled from his lips."

* * * * * *

There was long silence in the waiting-room after the K.A.R. officer had finished his story. Suddenly the far-away whistle of an approaching train echoed faintly. The four men stretched their cramped limbs and gathered up their belongings.

"Good heavens!" said the imaginative commercial traveler, as they stepped out into the cold grey light of dawn. "And you people are going back to it all, while I shall still be peddling my samples up and down the road. Dear God! to think of all I've missed in life."

VIII
THROUGH THE MIRROR

FIVE PIPES GLOWED REDLY in the semi-darkness. There was deep content beneath the thick thatch of the verandah at the back of Bruce Logan's summer bungalow. No one seemed inclined for conversation and only the gurgling of the pipes and the occasional sibilant hiss of soda water squirted from a syphon, or the clink of ice against the side of a tumbler, disturbed the silence.

Presently an owl called eerily, and immediately a dog-fox barked in the copse across the river. A refulgent, amber glow showed faintly above the far hills. Soon the rim of a big yellow harvest moon pushed up over the edge of the horizon. It was a night to awaken the memory and set the wanderer spinning camp-fire yarns.

As the moon rode clear of the ragged fringe of pine-trees upon the hills Logan turned to Colonel Rawden, who sat at his right.

"One can well imagine oneself back in Africa, with a moon of that size and colour in the heavens. Don't you think so, sir?" he queried.

"Indeed, yes," assented the soldier. "And, old as I am, I'd give all my back pay and pension to be out with my *Hausas* again, on the West Coast."

"I know very little of the West Coast, but I've had some varied experiences in East and Central Africa," said Bruce. "Some day I hope to go out to your part of the Continent, for I hear that experiences there are apt to be more varied than elsewhere, and my craving for adventure has never yet been satisfied."

"Well, if you don't get it cured on the West Coast I'm afraid you're a hopeless case," laughed the colonel.

As he paused to relight his pipe a fragment of conversation came to them from the far corner of the verandah, where Jack Spenser and Alderson, the barrister, who had made his name famous in the criminal courts, were leaning over the railing looking down into the valley, where the mist lay like a silvery carpet above the fields fringing the river.

"But surely," Jack was saying, "many of our antiquated statutes might nowadays be dispensed with?"

"It is surprising how few of them we could do without," replied Alderson. "For example, we found that old one which sets forth the penalties for slave trading very useful a few years ago."

"Why, how was that?" asked Hugh Trent, who was stretched at his ease in a tropical chair, the curve of which fitted his length of limb to a nicety.

"It is a long yarn," replied Alderson, "and the colonel would be the best one to tell it, since he was the principal witness at the trial. I wish you'd tell it, Rawden," he added, walking across to where Bruce Logan and the old soldier were seated. "I am quite sure there are a lot more details than you gave us in court."

"Well, maybe there are," said the colonel, with a reminiscent chuckle, "but I'm a poor hand at spinning a yarn."

"Never mind that, sir," said Jack. "Bruce has fired our imagination with many an African tale and we'd like very much to hear something about the West Coast from you."

"All right," said the colonel, "I'll see what I can do."

For a moment he sat thoughtful, filling his pipe, as he conjured up pictures from the past of the happenings he was about to relate.

"Fifteen, or maybe twenty, years ago," he said, "the Commissioner of the District in which I was stationed went down with blackwater fever and died. As it happened there was no other Commissioner, or Assistant Commissioner, available at the time to fill the post; and so the mantle of authority fell temporarily upon my shoulders, until such time as a new man could arrive from home to take the place of one of the Assistants, who would, in due course, be promoted to the vacant Commissionership.

"From headquarters there arrived, by special messenger, a large, red-sealed envelope in which reposed a parchment addressed to: 'Our well-beloved Frederick Rice Rawden, Captain, of our 9th/1st Norfolk Regiment, seconded for service in our 4th Regiment of *Hausas*—Greeting.' This was my commission and permission to take up the reins of government of an ever uneasy land, the size and inaccessibility of which would amaze you, if you cared to study a topographical map in comparison with a map of the British Isles drawn to the same scale.

"Things had been quiet in the district for a good many months. Inter-tribal fighting seemed to have well-nigh died out, crops were good, the riverine people reported good fishing, killing palavers were few and far between, and there had been no trouble in collecting the last levy of taxation. In these circumstances I felt justified in hoping that the 'machinery of State' would run smoothly until the new Commissioner arrived to rewind it; I hoped this most devoutly, for I am essentially a soldier, not an administrator. But at the back of my mind I had the uncomfortable feeling that big trouble was brewing.

"A month before the Commissioner's death—I was away at the time—carrier pigeons had come in bearing messages written upon the flimsiest of paper which had sent him—Arkwright his name was—flying up the river post haste.

"I never knew the contents of those 'books,'* for Arkwright had gone before I got back.

"A month later, when I was sitting one evening upon the verandah of the Residency, I caught the splash of paddles around the bend of the river and heard the voices of the paddlers singing the death chant.

"A moment later a canoe shot into sight. As they turned her, with deft strokes, into the bank I could distinguish the form of a

---

* On the West Coast everything which is written is referred to by the natives as a "book."

white man, partly hidden beneath a canopy of palm-leaves. Hastening down to the river, I was horrified to recognise poor Arkwright, who was quite evidently *in extremis*.

"I had him carried up to the Residency and did all that it was possible to do; but I knew from the first that his was a hopeless case.

"He lasted through the night, sometimes babbling quietly of home, at others raving wildly of lonely fights he had fought in the African jungle on his country's service against sloth, disease, and indifference. Towards morning he opened his eyes and I saw at once that he was no longer delirious.

"As I leaned over him he strove painfully, desperately, to speak, but his vocal chords seemed paralysed. At last two words were literally torn from his throat; they were 'Slaves! Ifambi!' and twice he forced them through his clenched teeth; then he died.

"One night some weeks later I was thinking of this as I sat alone at my unvarying dinner of chicken, palm oil chop, and the eternal rice pudding, which my soul loathed.

"Suddenly I was aware of a dark form waiting silently upon the verandah, just beyond the rays of lamplight which streamed out through the open window.

"'What want you, oh man?' I asked.

"'Master, a bird has brought a book,' answered Ahmet, my *Hausa* sergeant, stepping forward into the lamplight and saluting.

"The flimsy bore but three words: 'Slaves—Ifambi—Kubakara.'

"For hours I puzzled over it.

"'Slaves' conveyed little to me, for the Governor had told me, time and again, that the trade was completely stamped out in the territories which had fallen under British influence. Nor could I make any more of 'Ifambi' and 'Kubakara,' the names of two places on the river far apart. Something, however, had evidently attracted the attention of one of Arkwright's spies and it was obviously my duty, as acting Commissioner, to find out what that 'something' might be.

"Taking Arkwright's last words in conjunction with the present message from one of his trusted spies, I reasoned it out that some dealing in slaves was either contemplated or actually taking place;

and that the traders were probably moving from Ifambi to Kubakara, if they had not already arrived there; alternatively, raids
might be contemplated or planned against both places; in any case
it seemed to me that my chance of ascertaining the true facts would
be better at Kubakara than elsewhere.

"It took me a week to reach the village. We arrived, my *Hausas*
and I, twenty-four hours too late to be of any use, for the tragedy
had already been consummated; nor was there one single person
left alive to tell us the details of what had happened; matters in
general we understood well enough by the evidence of our own eyes.

"In the killing of the chief they had employed four young bam-
boo saplings; his head-men had died in various other unpleasant
ways. But there had undoubtedly been a brisk fight, for there were
a number of dead warriors amongst the smouldering remains of
the burnt-out huts, as well as the corpses of the old men and women
and the weaklings, with whom the raiders could not be bothered.

"From Kubakara we followed the trail, as broad as a cart road,
through the bush; only to find it returning, upon the curve of an
ellipse, to the river higher up. Greatly wondering at the motive
which had prompted this apparently meaningless march, I sent for
my canoes and pushed on to Ifambi.

"The journey took a week, and again we arrived within four-
and-twenty hours of the disaster. And again the evidence was all
too plain of the callous brutality of the slave traders. I judged from
the sight, indeed, that the leader of the raid must be a natural killer,
what is termed a 'homicidal maniac' among civilised peoples. He
had experimented devilishly upon many of his victims before death
had released them from his barbarity.

"This time I ignored the freshly-trampled road which led inland from the village and sent my servants flying up river in canoes, to ascertain where this road impinged upon the bank. At the
end of six hours they returned without information. I then followed
the slave road, only to find the same elliptical return to the banks
of the river, but below the village this time.

"Again I was puzzled, for why should the raiders deliberately
put my armed force between themselves and safety?

"The answer was awaiting me when we reached my coastwise headquarters. Two days before many canoes, heavily laden with slaves, had embarked their human cargo aboard a fleet of dhows which had put into the anchorage that morning.

"I wired at once to Administration H.Q., for the raid had evidently been planned by a master brain, which had calculated every least detail with the most meticulous care.

"A week later a British cruiser deposited the new Commissioner and two lady missionaries upon the shore. The former was a stern, hard-looking man, who had served a long apprenticeship in the tropics, and who appeared somewhat soured through long waiting for promotion. The latter were two sweet, clear-complexioned English girls fresh from home; tremendously enthusiastic about their work, but with no knowledge of the natives and the merest smattering of the native language. They were all on fire to proceed straight up country, but this the Commissioner flatly refused to allow, sending instead orders to the local chief to have suitable huts built for their reception.

"The elder of the two, Mrs. Stevens, was a widow, whose sole interest in life seemed to lie in her work; the other, Hilda Tredegar, was equally enthusiastic, but keenly interested in many other matters.

"During the month that the missionaries spent at the Residency Hilda and I saw much of each other, as was but natural. I did my best to persuade her to abandon missionary work in favour of matrimony, but she seemed to feel that she had a duty to God to perform, and nothing would shake her determination to go through with it.

"At the Commissioner's request I accompanied the missionaries up country and saw them installed in their new quarters.

"'B'Sano,' I said to the Chief of Ilumbi upon the day of my departure, 'these women are of my house, therefore you shall serve them well, guarding them with your life if need be.'

"'On my head and on my heart, master,' he answered, and I knew that I had done wisely to speak thus to him, for he was well disposed to the Government and had sworn the oath which no

follower of the Prophet will willingly break. For this reason I returned to the coast, feeling somewhat more easy in my mind than
would otherwise have been the case.

"Two months passed, and the reports which arrived from the
missionaries at Ilumbi told of few converts, but a pleasant enough
life in the tropical garden they were making. Then no word came
at all.

"'I think, Rawden,' said the Commissioner one night, when we
were seated together upon the verandah, 'that you had better go to
Ilumbi and see how things are going there. I don't like this prolonged silence and yet my spies are in the district and there should
be news if anything is wrong.

"Next morning I started by canoe for Ilumbi, accompanied by
Sergeant Ahmet and a dozen *Hausas.*

"At the villages we passed upon our journey the people seemed
strangely apprehensive, but I could get no information from them.

"'Man.' said I to one chief, 'what is it that makes all the people
afraid?'

"'Master, it is *Ewa,*' he answered.

"Then I knew that there was trouble ahead indeed, for *Ewa*
means 'death.'

"I should have turned back then for reinforcements, but I was
anxious for the women at Ilumbi and so pushed on.

"With Ilumbi less than two miles distant a thin spiral of smoke
showed above the forest, just about where I judged the village to
stand; the river, usually thronged with fisher-folk at that hour—it
was sunset—was absolutely deserted. I felt distinctly apprehensive.
Nor did it make things better when old Sergeant Ahmet shuddered
suddenly, and in answer to my look of interrogation answered:—

"'*Ewa, Effendi.* I can feel it near me!'

"The men paddled on in dead silence for awhile; then, just as
the river swung round in a bend and the village came in sight,
Ahmet trembled again.

"It is close now, *Effendi,*' he whispered, but none the less settled
himself stoically upon the little saddle of the Maxim gun which
was mounted forward.

"We passed the fringe of trees masking the bend, and fire seemed to leap at us from every quarter. The crash was deafening, but I heard poor old Ahmet cough, as he pitched forward on to the gun which had been the pride of his life. At the same instant I felt a violent blow, followed by a sharp pain. Nor did it take me long to realise that my collar bone was shattered. Then the boat went under in a welter of boiling water.

"When I came to myself I was hanging in bonds; supported thereby and lashed fast to a stake in the centre of the village of Ilumbi.

"Across the square a great train of slaves, already yoked together, was being driven away into the bush, the slave-drivers' whips cracking viciously and cutting the raw flesh from the black backs of the natives 'with every flick of the hippo lashes. My God! it was damnable, and the sight of it made me stiffen instinctively in my bonds. As I lifted my head I heard a mocking laugh.

"'The sight of my "blackbirds" displeases the soldier?' asked a suave voice in Arabic.

"I tried hard to see who had spoken, but the man evidently stood behind the stake.

"Presently he strolled around in front, and I was surprised to see that he was smoking a cigarette.

"'Your following was woefully small for the business on hand,' he said. 'I have often noticed that you English over-rate your powers and take the most foolish risks. This was so in '52, when you faced the Russians, and again in '57, when you had the Indian Mutiny on your hands.'

"I stared at him in mute amazement, for, although he spoke faultless Arabic, this was not the reasoning of an Arab.

"Having made sure that my curiosity was thoroughly aroused, he left me. I stood there, leaning against the stake, wondering what had become of the missionaries and considering my own position; since it was obvious that in bonds I could give them no aid even if they still lived. Having formed my judgment of the Arab leader, I am free to confess that I hoped they were already dead."

Colonel Rawden knocked out the "dottle" of his pipe against the rail of the verandah and slowly refilled and lit it. He took a long pull from the tumbler which stood at his elbow, as if preparing himself for what was to come; he stopped down the glowing tobacco in the bowl of his pipe, and continued his story.

"All of you have been through war," he said. "You know how long a man can live in hell and keep his reason, but that night provided such a concentrated essence of horror as I dare not repeat to even such war-hardened soldiers as you. But I can tell you one thing, I was perfectly right in my surmise that the leader of the slave traders was a killer by nature.

"Towards dawn that fiend in human shape came across to where I stood in my bonds.

"'Well, what do you think of my little experiments?' he asked.

"That my answer shamed even his own black soul I like still to think, for I am a good linguist so far as Arabic and the native dialects are concerned, and I packed all the concentrated loathing and contempt I felt into the few sentences he allowed me to speak before he slashed me across the mouth with the handle of his heavy whip.

"'I have not done with you yet,' he said quite quietly, but for all that I could see that he was boiling over with rage.

"Then, oh my God! then he had Hilda and her fellow missionary led into the square, where men and women were still writhing in the agony of death.

"'These,' he said, 'will accompany me when I go hence, but first I shall build you in and light a slow fire, and after that I shall leave you to roast.'

"For one moment my eyes met Hilda's and, although no word was spoken, I knew that I had not loved her in vain. Then they yoked her with Mrs. Stevens, and I heard the whips crack as they were driven off.

"The Arab stood before me, smiling evilly, and every lineament of his features beneath the close-drawn white head-cloth was indelibly imprinted upon my memory.

"'Man,' I said, 'if I survive this affair I will hunt you down and bring you to death, though I have to seek you in the uttermost parts of the earth.'

"'You will not find me,' he answered, 'for this is my last raid, and the price of the white women will be high in the market where I shall sell them.'

"For a moment he stood still, listening intently; he clapped a whistle to his lips; at the shrill blast his few remaining followers, personal servants mostly, came running swiftly. Together they made their way across the square and disappeared among the huts.

"Shortly after I heard the chug-chug of a motor-boat upon the river.

"Then I think I must have fainted. At any rate, I knew no more until I came to and found the friendly face of the Commissioner leaning above me.

"'It's all right, Rawden,' he said. 'I got a message by pigeon as to what was afoot and came up post haste with the rest of your detachment of *Hausas*.'

"'But the women,' I asked, 'what of the women?'

"'I am afraid,' answered the Commissioner, 'that our only hope is that they may find a quick and easy means of death.'

"Within five hours I was off with my company of *Hausas* in pursuit of the Arabs, and this time there was no chance of their doubling back upon their own tracks to the water; for the Commissioner, with a couple of Maxim guns mounted in the bows of his canoes, patrolled the river.

"We moved by forced marches, making better pace than I ever remember, even for African native troops, who are notoriously fast marchers and capable, moreover, of sticking out their thirty miles a day, day in, day out. It was evident that the traders knew we were after them, for we found many a poor wretch who had fallen by the track from sheer exhaustion and who had been ruthlessly butchered lest information should be given.

"By dawn the next day I was hard put to it to keep going, for my shoulder was infernally painful and I could literally feel my temperature rising. At mid-morning we heard the whips cracking ahead and spread our line out fanwise in an enveloping movement.

"The fight that followed was short and sharp and there was no quarter either given or asked for, but still I did manage at the last to find a couple of Kano men alive, but desperately wounded.

"Neither threats, promises, nor persuasion would make them talk. No word would they say of where their leader had gone, nor whence he had come; but from the people of B'Sano's village I learned the details of the raid and of how greatly the chief and the last of his warriors had fallen in defence of the white women; but of the missionaries themselves I could get no news; they had never joined the slave train.

"After I had returned the people of Ilumbi to their village and the Commissioner had appointed a new chief, we returned to the coast.

"When I had recovered from my wound I applied for and got six months' leave of absence and, fitting out my own expedition, set out to track down the Arab and his captives.

"I will not weary you with the details of that search, for it was absolutely unavailing. The party which had made good its escape in the motor-boat might have vanished into thin air for all the news I could get of them; but on every hand I heard spoken of a mysterious white man who had appeared alone from the unknown interior on his way to the coast; but curiously enough, the Commissioner had seen nothing of this man when I arrived back at the Residency.

"It may sound a strange thing to say, but I had a feeling of absolute certainty that sooner or later I should find that infernal slave trader and, for that reason I would not leave Africa; indeed, I did not come home except on intermittent leave until the war broke out. Then I returned to my old line regiment to get the best of the fighting.

"When the Somme advance began in 1916 I was at Gommecourt, after that I was a year in hospital, after that again a Medical Board decided that I was only fit for staff employment in England and so a job was found for me at the War Office.

"There is, as you are probably aware, a hair-dressing saloon just off Piccadilly which is very popular with Service men and there were not many days in the week when I did not drop in there, for one reason or another.

"In November, when things were moving rapidly overseas, we old staff-wallahs were pretty well pushed to death and I remember one anxious period when we were at it night and day. On my way to Whitehall after one all-night sitting, I dropped into Skipton's for a hot toweling, which I thought might freshen me up for another's day work.

"The saloon was absolutely packed. I was too tired to read the papers with which the seats were littered and so I sat and studied the people around me while I was waiting.

"The man in the barber's hands immediately in front of me was having a wet shampoo, and presently the attendant wrapped a towel round his head and drew him upright.

"Instantly a tragically familiar face started out at me from the mirror.

"There was the same white cloth drawn tight about the brow, the same crafty eyes, thin nose and cruel mouth, which I had last seen sneering at me as I stood bound to the stake in the African village of Ilumbi; but this man's skin was white, therefore I might not have recognised him but for the chance of the towel drawn tight about his brow and the dark flush with which the hot water had suffused his countenance.

"I made no sign of recognition, although I felt as though my brain would burst with fierce joy. I looked casually at my watch as if tired of waiting and walked quietly out.

"Once in the street I looked around for a constable. I was lucky enough to run into an inspector whom I knew slightly and of course, my position as a staff colonel gave me a good deal of prestige, so that I had little difficulty in arranging for the man's detention on suspicion."

"And what was the outcome of it all, colonel?" asked Bruce, who never by any possible chance read the newspapers.

"Eh!" said the colonel. "Surely you have heard how Alderson here, acting as Crown Prosecutor, drew out the story of how this fellow, Clive Mattison, had been expelled from school for bullying, and later sent down from the 'Varsity for the most horrible brutality to a cat he caught in his rooms, after which his people disowned him and he drifted out to Africa, where his lust for cruelty had so completely carried him away that he had turned slave trader. But I don't think he had ever really realised what suffering was until our friend here put him under cross-examination and showed him himself in the eyes of the world. At the last he broke down and confessed to the murder of Mrs. Stevens and Hilda Tredegar, and on that count they hanged him for the killer he undoubtedly was."

"Yes," interposed the barrister, "but we'd have had him on the old statute prohibiting the slave trade just the same, even if he hadn't made a more or less voluntary confession."

IX
AFTER MANY YEARS

IT IS A FINE THING to be the only son of a successful financier, to have placed to your credit every quarter-day a substantial sum for the performance of purely nominal duties as one's father's secretary.

This was the good fortune of man named Warboys, a young man bred up in idleness, but of considerable personality.

Unfortunately, the father over-reached himself in the matter of speculation and, in consequence, committed suicide; he left "all my real and personal estate to my beloved and only son, John Christian Warboys," but that estate amounted to rather less than £400, a sum which inadequately compensated John Christian for the substantial payment which hitherto had been placed to his credit at the bank each quarter with clocklike regularity.

He had, moreover, a charming wife and a wonderful baby, whose demands upon his resources were by no means small.

A financier's secretary of small practical experience, and who is above every form of sharp practice, is a drug on the market, which distrusts financiers and all their satellites. Young Warboys spent a year and most of his capital before he came to realise that his services were unsaleable.

If the father had made soap or candles of a special excellence, and if before blowing out his brains he had imparted to his son the family secret of the formula whereby these commodities were made, young Warboys would have had no difficulty in finding employment. Had he had a proper business training he might have found his particular niche in the world of commerce; but he had specialised in keeping his father good-tempered, and the world had no openings for his undoubted good qualities, unbacked by specific, technical knowledge. He had exactly £400 of his savings and inheritance left when this fact dawned upon him.

Then it happened that, sitting by the fire in their suburban home one evening, Irma, his wife, mentioned her grandfather—he had been an adventurous explorer and treasure-seeker—who had gone finally into the interior of Africa in search of a well-authenticated, and equally well-hidden, treasure, from which search neither he nor his companions had ever returned.

Warboys asked for further information, and Irma fetched an old deed box, which had not been opened for many years.

"These are the plans and papers," she said, "which the family solicitor gave to me after my father's death."

John and his pretty wife sat up till the early hours of the morning discussing the possibility of the treasure being there. They pored over the old explorer's rough map, which showed a river flowing from a swamp in the interior to the coast, and precious little else besides. The country bordering the river upon either bank was shown as dense bush or entirely unexplored. There were a few big hills, but apparently no permanent villages. But, according to the manuscript which accompanied the map, the country had once been inhabited by a powerful Persian race, who had been exterminated by the nomadic Somalis; but not before the national treasure had been buried in a hill marked "Sereda." This hill was shown impinging upon the right bank of the river, marked "Lak Dera," and surrounded upon every other side by dense jungle.

Further inquiry from outside sources elicited the facts that the river, which must be followed before the treasure could be reached, was frequently dried up, that the country was unhealthy, the thermometer standing usually at about 115 degrees in the shade, while the sole inhabitants were said to be peculiarly vicious mosquitoes—of a non-malaria carrying species, however; wild beasts and the Mohammed Zubhier Somalis, who had massacred the last exploration party at a place called Liboyi, some two hundred miles inland from Kismayu and fifty miles short of Sereda Hill. It was believed that no white man had ever penetrated further into the interior than Liboyi.

"Then how do you account for the existence of the map which has descended to my wife from her grandfather, Herbert Strangeways?" asked Warboys of the Royal Geographical Society official, to whom he had gone for advice upon the matter.

"He had it in all probability from the Lamus or the Bajun people of the islands off Kismayu, who claim descent from the Persians," answered the official.

"It seems a dreadfully dangerous country," said Irma when her husband told her all that he had learned.

Warboys shook his head doubtfully.

"There is no opening for me in this country," he said, "and if I don't earn some money soon we shall starve."

They went into the cost of the expedition and found that if he traveled second class and practised the most rigid economy it could be done. He could leave her £150; sufficient to last her, with care, for twelve months.

He sailed from Liverpool, and, as the fluttering handkerchief of his wife grew to an indistinct white speck, he realised that there are more bitter things in life than death.

He changed his ship at Durban and again at Mombassa, where he found accommodation on a small coasting steamer, which landed him at Lamu the following evening.

At Lamu he stayed a few days making diligent but guarded inquiry for anyone who had known Herbert Strangeways, or who could tell him more than he already knew concerning the Sereda treasure.

That the people were of the descent to which they laid claim he fully believed, for the ruins of ancient mosques and stone houses which fringed the coast line were unmistakably Persian in design. But the present inhabitants of Lamu and the Bajun Islands either would not or could not tell him anything.

The day after he left Lamu he reached Kismayu, which is now the seat of government for Jubaland.

The Provincial Commissioner went down to meet the steamer, which sometimes brought the mails, and to him John was introduced by the skipper.

Mr. Commissioner Saltmarsh raised his eyebrows when he heard that the young man proposed making a stay at Kismayu, which, even to-day, comprises but a few stone houses and a not inconsiderable number of native huts, but which was much smaller at the time of which I write.

In the Commissioner's verandah over coffee that evening John spoke without reserve.

"I've come out here to get the Sereda Hill treasure," he said frankly. "There was no opening for me at home, and I've got to make a fortune, or, at any rate, a living, somehow."

"You've hit upon the unhealthiest and least likely way of doing it," answered Saltmarsh with a smile.

"Yes; but the possibilities pretty well justify the risk, I fancy," replied the other.

Then, making no secret of his slender means and still smaller experience, he told his story.

Saltmarsh was interested. The picture of the struggle to make good in a vast, unsympathetic community was strange and unpleasant to him. His sympathy was awakened.

"You've had the most appalling kind of luck," he said kindly; "but still I feel that I ought to advise you to throw up this mad treasure hunt, only I'm pretty sure you would not take my advice."

"No," answered John, "I can't go back, because, you see, I have broken down all the bridges behind me!"

"I wish I could find you a job here," said the Commissioner.

"That's very good of you," answered John; "but I'd rather you gave me permission to travel inland, and some advice as to fitting out the expedition."

Saltmarsh smiled as he pushed a decanter across the table to his guest.

"Have it your own way," he said; "you've determination enough to carry you through. But don't be disappointed if you do get to Sereda Hill and find the treasure gone or non-existent."

He wrote out the necessary permission next day.

For ten days the young man was busy assembling his *safari*. The caravan consisted of eighteen camels and twenty-four men, including a small escort of native police. The Commissioner armed the party with rifles, since it was more than probable that the Somalis, who pasture their great herds of cattle inland, would prove hostile. He lent John ten of the large copper water tanks, without which travel in Jubaland is impossible. He also found a head-man and an interpreter for him; and the young man set off to seek a fortune, after writing a letter to his wife, in which he called down the blessings of Heaven upon Saltmarsh.

Before he went Saltmarsh gave him a few words of advice.

"You will find patience, perseverance and firmness your best friends," he said; "above all, keep your temper. You will be traveling through trackless and, in many parts, waterless wastes. You will find the country so thick with bush in some regions that it will appear almost impossible to hack a way through, but if you keep your men up to concert-pitch you will find they can work wonders with those large chopping knives, called *pangas*, which they have at their belts.

"The Ogaben Somalis you are sure to meet. They are unfriendly to white men and very treacherous. But your main trouble will be the water supply. You will be told of a place where water is obtainable. That place may be anything from twenty-five to a hundred miles from where you are. By the time you reach it, after innumerable difficulties, your water tanks will be at least half empty; if the drinking place is dry you will have a nice problem to face.

"As I have said, your tanks will be getting empty; your men, after the fatigue of cutting out every foot of your road through the bush, will be discontented, if not actually mutinous; in addition to which they will be 'jumpy,' knowing as they do that the young Somali warrior is always seeking trouble, because he desires to assume the *bal*—the feathered head dress—which signifies that he has slain a man in fight. The next water supply will be not less than fifty miles further on, and you will have to make up your mind whether you will turn back to safety, when I will find you some sort of a job here, or go on and risk it. If you go on and find water you will be all right. If the water is not forthcoming it is the end, for you will die of thirst.

"I'm afraid it's not a very encouraging prospect, but it is only fair to warn you. Good-bye and good luck."

He watched the long line of silent-footed camels disappear into the desert and went back to his office, where he entered the departure in his diary.

Journeying up to Afmadu, John met many of the Galla people, who let him pass unchallenged; but it was not until he reached Jeldez, some hundred miles inland, that he fell in with the nomadic Somalis, the first of whom he saw through his binoculars early one morning.

Working his way cautiously forward through some low scrub, John was able to observe the man closely. He was at prayer.

Presently he rose, and, taking from his belt a light stick, to the end of which was attached a tuft of marabou feathers, tested the wind. He then produced another stick some two feet long and hollow, through which he sucked up water from a deep cleft in the rock. The rest of his equipment consisted of a round shield made of giraffe's hide, which was strapped to his left arm, a short, broad-bladed spear and a horn-handled dagger, a tooth-stick and a wonderfully carved wooden pillow, which was strapped to his left wrist. John noticed, moreover, that the man's spear shaft was of black wood, not unlike ebony, which indicated that he had killed an enemy of his tribe.

Soon the man mounted his camel and rode slowly forward, peering out in all directions under his curved palm. John judged him to be a scout, and lay still to see if any more of his people would materialise.

Shortly after other scouts passed his hiding-place, and presently a vast mixed herd of cattle, camels, sheep and goats were driven past under escort in the direction of Jeldez. Then came the tribe, with a long string of camels, each bearing a load of mats woven from grass and three curved poles on either side to complete a primitive pack saddle; between the poles were piled the household goods, while little children, slung in sacks and balanced on the other side by tiny lambs' or goats' kids, completed the load.

Close to John's hiding-place the caravan halted and made camp. Huts, indescribably squalid in appearance, were constructed by driving six of the curved posts into the ground; the tops were then tied together and the whole structure covered with grass mats, only the smallest openings being left for the occupants to come in and out and for the smoke to escape.

John was about to creep away, back through the thorn scrub to his own caravan, when a weight fell upon him, pinning him to the ground.

In a moment his hands were bound. He was driven forward at the point of a spear into the Somali camp, where he was thrust into a hut and, much to his surprise, given food, consisting of milk, ghee and rice.

Towards evening he was taken again into the open, where he found the men of the tribe sitting around, evidently awaiting the commencement of some tribal ceremony.

Now, as he learned later, the Jubaland Somalis are strict Mussulmen, who will not, therefore, touch any form of alcohol, but have a beverage of their own called *buni*. This Somaliland coffee must be partaken of by all present before any important matter, be it dance, discussion or decision, can be dealt with.

"My son," said the Somali chief to John, "you are a stranger in our land, whose purpose we know not; before we ask it let us sit and partake of the *buni*, which makes glad the heart, clear the brain and strong the limbs, after even the greatest fatigue."

John sat down, an interested spectator.

He saw the coffee berries fried whole in ghee. The latter was then poured off into a dish, which was solemnly handed to the chief, who passed it on to the next man, and so it went from man to man in order of age. Each dipped his hand into the dish, thereafter anointing head, face or arms with the hot ghee, according to his fancy. Meanwhile, the coffee berries were being boiled in a saturated solution of sugar and water, to which a little more ghee was added. This sticky mess the Somalis drank greedily, but the first sip of it very nearly made John sick.

While the *buni* drinking was in progress, John's brain was busy, striving to concoct a plausible excuse for his presence in that place. But the time for explanations was not yet come, for a messenger arrived and whispered something to the chief, after which all was hurry and bustle. The camels were loaded to the rhythm of a monotonous song and soon the caravan moved off in the moonlight, until Jeldez was reached, and the same song was sung while the camels were off-loaded. Then came the "Song of Thanksgiving" because, after a long march, water had been reached at last.

That night, for they had arrived at dawn, there was a great war dance, and it may be remarked, incidentally, that the Somalis know no form of musical instrument, not even the tom-tom, so dear to the heart of most natives.

It was the season of the full moon and no other light was needed when the chief seated himself, with John standing beside him, to watch the dance.

In the very centre of the dancing place was stretched an ox-hide, and close to it waited twelve chosen warriors, armed with spear, shield and knife and wearing their sandals.

The well at Jeldez is in the centre of a depression, some three hundred yards in diameter, and the top of it marks the edge of the dense surrounding bush. Upon the slopes the spectators waited in circles, the outermost ring being composed of the women.

There was a long pause of hushed expectation.

A signal was given, whereat the twelve warriors began to sing and then to dance in a circle, which decreased gradually, until the twelve were stamping together upon the ox-hide. Suddenly a young warrior, newly crowned with the *bal*, rushed towards the chief, leaping an incredible height into the air, brandishing his spear and finally saluting; one after another of his companions followed his example; as one man rushed forward alone the other eleven stamped altogether upon the ox-hide. Faster and faster they danced and more wildly leapt into the air.

As the frenzy increased the spectators joined in, the men stamping their feet upon the hard ground in time to the song, while the women in the outer ring urged on the twelve leaping warriors with weird, high yells, the savagery of which simply beggars description.

John, who at first had been carried away by the weird novelty of the spectacle, soon noticed that the glances leveled at him grew more and more hostile as the pace increased; at last all eyes were centred upon him. Nor was it long before the people were clamouring openly for his blood.

"Peace, peace!" shouted the chief. "We know not whence the white man comes nor why." And after that he caused John to be led back to his hut, lest the sight of him should enrage the people beyond control.

For this opportune intervention John was truly thankful, but he was sensible that it was but a respite that had been given him, and that unless he could either escape or arouse the Somalis' interest in the treasure his chances of living through another four and twenty hours were very slender. In any case he did not think his situation could very well have been worse. Should he escape, the probability was that he would find his caravan had already set off upon the return journey to Kismayu; if, on the other hand, he should tell the Somali chief of the treasure, he felt tolerably certain that his throat would be slit once that treasure had been found.

For awhile he worked desperately, but without avail, to loosen his bonds; but, his wrists became so swollen that the rope was almost hidden from sight and he was forced to desist; after a while he fell into a troubled sleep.

Presently it seemed to him that a Hindoo, clad in the white garments, snowy turban and scarlet *cummerbund* of the *khitmatghar*, stood before him. He moved his limbs and he found himself free. Outside he saw the sentry squatted upon his heels asleep, his back resting against one of the curved poles of the hut.

Following the silent Hindoo through the sleeping camp John came to the place where the camels were picketed. One—a fine beast, of the true Bisharin racing strain—was kneeling by itself ready saddled. This he mounted at a sign from the Hindoo, who still had not spoken.

An instant later the young man felt as though he were being broken in half as the beast heaved itself up in sections. A stick was in his hands, with which he tapped the slender, snake-like neck before him, as he had seen the Somalis do. The camel shot forward like an express train, racing along the forest path up which the caravan had previously passed. John had neither need nor opportunity to use the stick again, all his attention being occupied in clinging to the horn of the saddle with hands and legs. Time and again through that awful ride he felt that his body must burst and he be disemboweled, for he had not the swathings about his stomach which the natives use when they ride the racing camel; but his will-power held him sentient until he reached the place where he had left his followers. He found them making ready to set out upon the return journey.

They were in a well-concealed position and close to water; the tanks had been recently filled, moreover, and there John decided to rest a week before projecting a further advance into the interior.

Meanwhile the pack-saddles, girths and ropes were overhauled and repaired. On the seventh day the caravan moved forward, passing Jeldez far to the north at about midday. Towards sunset a thick "wait-a-bit" belt was entered; the short, strongly curved thorns played havoc with the loads and caused John to swear fluently on account of the delay; but at 2 a.m. or thereabouts he heard frogs croaking, and knew that he was nearing the pools, called by the natives "Roble," which means "The Pools of Rainwater."

Of these two pools he found one dry and the other containing but a little very foul water, covered with star-shaped water lilies. There was nothing for it but to push on. This he did, reaching Liboyi, where a previous expedition had been massacred, towards noon upon the next day.

Here fresh trouble arose, for of the two dozen men who composed the caravan all but one refused to go farther. The one exception was the head-man, who was himself one of the Maghabul Somalis—a small section of the Ogaben tribe claiming descent from an Arab sheik said to have settled on the Benadir coast in 1300 A.D.

John was unwilling that the men who had traveled with him so far should starve or die of thirst in the desert, wherefore he gave them the majority of the camels and six water tanks, also a letter to Mr. Commissioner Saltmarsh, which, as he assured Jubatalla, the Maghabul Somali, and as in due course the renegades found to their cost, "contained many beatings."

These two then pushed on alone, traversing first a fertile country of rich alluvial soil bordering the Lak Aboloni, but entering subsequently a vast expanse of low thorn scrub, uninhabited and practically waterless. This tract the Somalis name "Rama," which in their language means "The Wilderness."

In this terrible place the expedition came almost to an end.

Crossing a rocky defile one of the camels fell, bursting the two water tanks it carried beyond any hope of repair; the other two tanks were at that time well-nigh empty, and, moreover, the thermometer stood at 116 deg. Fahrenheit, so that the men's throats were soon dry and their lips cracked and blistered.

"Master," whispered Jubatalla, whose tongue was very swollen, "it is my thought that we shall die in this place; for the Lak Dera is dry at this season, and Chimbirlre—the 'Pool of Birds'—more than twenty miles away. Is it your will that I kill one of the camels that we may take the water from its stomach?"

"No," answered John grimly. "We'll stick it out a bit longer yet. We may be lucky enough to find a rock pool of rainwater. I shall want the camels, if ever we reach Sereda Hill."

"The hill is very close to the 'Pool of Birds,'" said Jubatalla resignedly.

For a while longer they struggled on, but John had over-estimated both his own powers of endurance and those of the desert-bred Somali. Nightfall found them lying unconscious by their patient beasts at the edge of the thorn scrub.

Once again it seemed to John that the silent Hindoo servant stood beside him, beckoning to him to follow. He turned and roused

Jubatalla, and together they stumbled forward, following the white figure which showed dimly in the veiled moonlight.

Presently the moon sailed out from behind a cloud, and they saw, some distance off, a gazelle about the size of a black-tailed deer, but which had a peculiarly long, giraffe-like neck. It was balanced cleverly upon its hind legs, browsing on the succulent leaves, far out of reach of all other species of buck.

"A gerenuk!" whispered Jubatalla. "He lives always near the water."

Together they stumbled on again, and presently saw a dark line of *waja* and flat-topped acacia trees rising high above the thorn scrub. Another half hour found them flat upon their faces drinking great draughts of clear water.

"The Pool of Birds," gasped the Somali as he stood up, wiping the water from his glistening skin. "We were nearer than I had thought."

And now, his thirst assuaged, John turned to tender his thanks to the Hindoo servant, but he had vanished.

"Jubatalla," said John, "where is the Mahindi who led us here?"

"Master," answered the Somali, "I saw no Mahindi."

Nor, when they searched at daylight, could they find any trace of the Hindoo's spoor.

Together they went back to the spot where they had left the camels hobbled overnight and found the distance comparatively short in their refreshed state. When they arrived the camels were struggling with their ropes and stretching out their necks towards the north-west in the direction of Chimbirlre, where it was evident the poor beasts had winded the water. They made a straight line for it at their best pace once they were released.

After a rest of twenty-four hours by the "Pool of Birds," John decided to finish the journey to Sereda Hill.

Traveling along the right bank of the almost dry Lak Dera, they avoided the densest part of the jungle, but found the route difficult enough, since the ground rose steeply towards the eight hundred feet high hill.

Once clear of the jungle tracts and with the crest of Sereda in sight, John's impatience knew no bounds; neither the eloquence of Jubatalla, nor the dictates of commonsense could persuade him to postpone the search until they had made camp and partaken of food.

When John returned weary, bruised and disappointed from the first fruitless essay, Jubatalla placed tea and a meal before his master, and, with due solemnity, prepared *buni* for himself.

After several times anointing his head and breast above the heart with the superfluous ghee, he drank the sickly mess to the last dregs.

John, who by this time was beginning to know a little about the Somalis, gathered from these proceedings that Jubatalla was rapidly arriving at an important decision, which he might be expected to communicate in due course.

At last the native spoke.

"Master," said he, "you have told me that you visit this land of Rama seeking a great treasure, the finding of which shall make you as a chief of chiefs among your own people."

"All that you say is true," John answered.

"And, master, one of your house came here aforetime from the land of the Mahindi (Hindoos) seeking also to gain this treasure; but, having committed his body to Rama, came back no more."

"Yes! What of it?"

"This, master; each time evil has befallen us and things have seemed at their worst, relief has come; and always afterwards you have asked me for news of a Mahindi whom you seemed to see."

"Yes, what of it?" asked John again.

"Nothing, master; only, if you do not succeed at first, do not despair; for it is my thought that the Mahindi, who comes of a race having strange powers, may show himself again."

For long enough John pondered over this conversation, of which he could make nothing, nor, cross-question him as he would, could he get the imperturbable Jubatalla to say another word.

There is no need to tell how, for a month and more, they explored Sereda Hill, for that search was unutterably wearisome and entirely disappointing. At last, when they had scarcely enough food left to see them back across the barren lands, where no game roams, John decided definitely to abandon the treasure hunt and to return as best he might to Kismayu; but beyond the return to the hospitality of Mr. Commissioner Saltmarsh he dared not think.

His wife and child at home could have barely enough money left to tide them over the next two months, while he himself had little more than his passage money back to England.

While Jubatalla struck the tent and made ready the camels upon that last morning, John took his rifle and strolled idly up the slope of the hill.

Suddenly a hartebeeste of a peculiar sort, in that the facial glands were extraordinarily developed and the beast showed an enormous roll of fat immediately behind the horns, leaped up before him and sped swiftly up the hill. Keenly alive to the fact that a new type of hartebeeste was escaping from him, and anxious, moreover, to obtain the meat which would help preserve their slender stock of tinned stuff, John threw up his rifle and fired. The beast went down, with his legs sprawling all ways at once, so that the hunter was virtually certain its back was broken; but, as he approached, it sprang up and made off, running strongly. Despite this, John was quite sure it was badly wounded, and, being unwilling to leave game he had hit to die a lingering death, followed the blood trail, for the buck was by this time out of sight.

Looking up presently from the spoor he was following he was surprised to find himself in totally unfamiliar surroundings, for he had thought by this time that he knew every nook and corner of Sereda Hill.

He crossed a ridge and stood looking down into a glen which was little more than a pit of shadows. The blood slot led downwards, and, though the descent was short, it was very steep. The undergrowth was not dense upon this slope, but promised foot and hand hold for an active man. But John had not been climbing more than two minutes before he wished that he had been content to leave the buck to its fate.

To his dismay he found that the slope, which had commenced gently enough, had become a precipice, and that while retreat was difficult, descent was equally perilous. For a moment he hung there, clasping a bush with both hands; suddenly his feet slipped, and at the same moment the bush, now called upon to bear his whole weight, came out by the roots.

When John regained consciousness he was lying upon a ledge of rock, with a head and limbs which ached terribly. He lay still for a long time, not daring to move in the impenetrable darkness and uncertain as to the extent of his injuries. Presently the yellow rim of the moon pushed up over the crest of Sereda. As the white light lit upon the cliff face down which he had fallen, John saw some twenty feet above his head a great gaping hole, which could hardly have been rent in the hillside by the uprooting of the bush which had precipitated his fall. Looking below him, John saw, some distance down, a huge boulder, and to it the bush was still attached by the roots; close by lay his rifle. At the bottom of the glen a rocky slope swept around the foot of the cliff towards the camp, where he knew Jubatalla would be anxiously awaiting his return.

He was pleased and not a little surprised to find that, for all his agony, no bones were broken. He lost no time in making ready to regain his rifle. He proposed following the sweep of the rocky outcrop back to his camp.

With due caution he made his way downwards and picked up his rifle. To his delight, he found that it was uninjured, although the cartridge had been fired by the fall. On the rocky ledge, broad as a first-class highway, he halted to reload his weapon. Before leaving the spot he looked up at the scene of the disaster and was amazed to see what he took to be the form of a man standing at the opening in the hillside whence the boulder had been dislodged. Then a big bank of clouds obscured the face of the moon and he could not be sure that it really was a human figure that he had seen. In breathless anxiety he waited, for he could not understand what any person could want in that desolate place and, moreover, he had a presentiment that a psychological moment had arrived. It seemed that the clouds would never pass, so slowly did they drift. He jumped nervously as a baboon barked and was answered again and yet again across the hillside. At last the moon rode clear, and then he seemed to see the figure of a Hindoo standing in the cave entrance above him. As he watched the man appeared to raise a beckoning hand, then he vanished.

John felt the sweat start out upon his limbs as he commenced to re-ascend the hill. As he approached the spot where he had met with disaster upon the previous night he was struck by the peculiar aspect of the ground. The bush he had uprooted and the boulder which had followed it could never have torn so great a cavity in the earth. It yawned like the mouth of a tunnel. He climbed nearer and saw that inside the cave the walls had been chiseled as by human hands, while the floor had been leveled and made smooth by the passage of many feet.

John seated himself upon what might well have been the last of a very ancient flight of descending stairs. He filled his pipe, and awaited the coming of dawn.

Always of a romantic turn of mind, he had been from the first inclined to the treasure hunt principally, but probably subconsciously, by the speculative and risky element which entered so largely into the undertaking. The past and the doings of dead generations held an undeniable fascination for him. Now, as he sat there awaiting the dawn, he conjured up pictures of those old-world Persian adventurers, who he felt sure had cut the steps, upon the last of which he sat, and had, moreover, climbed down them very many times to hide their treasure in the cave. One vision in particular persisted; it was that of a young man falling down the cliff face and again climbing upwards with a look of set purpose in his eyes. Laughing at himself and his fancies, John knocked out his pipe, then he rose and entered the cave.

For thirty feet or more the shaft was driven straight into the hillside and then turned abruptly to the right through a curiously carved arch, upon the surface of which the figures of men and beasts showed indistinctly in the dim light. In almost total darkness John went forward, with a hand feeling the walls of the passage on either side. Suddenly his fingers closed on naught but space.

He fumbled in his pocket, and found a box of matches. He struck one and saw that he was in a vast chamber, the walls of which were

lined with tier upon tier of great chests. By the light of a second
match he saw that one of these chests had burst, allowing a great
stream of flashing jewels and golden coins to flow out upon the
floor. That match was his last and it was not until he had returned
to the camp for lanterns and Jubatalla that John was able to ex-
plore the great treasure cave thoroughly.

All that day was spent in examining the vast store of wealth
which was hidden in the hillside.

"Jubatalla," said John, "you alone of all the *safari* have proved
faithful, but you will be well rewarded, for your share of this treasure will make you the greatest chief from coast to coast."

"But, master, now that Allah in His mercy has given the reward, how shall we get it away?"

"Listen," John answered; "we will take with us of the best jewels and gold coins as much as the camels can carry, afterwards
we will close the entrance to the cave; and then I will go back to
England to get money for the jewels, after which I will return and
fit out a well-protected *safari*, big enough to come here and get
the rest; and you shall await me at Kismayu, saying nothing of the
treasure to any man."

"On my head and on my heart, I will be silent," answered the
Somali.

Towards nightfall, when they had collected as much treasure
as the camels could carry and were preparing to leave the cave, a
sudden exclamation of surprise broke from John's lips. In pushing aside an almost empty box he had discovered a small doorway
cut in the living rock and closed. He called to Jubatalla to bring
the lamp.

A strange sight awaited him when he opened the door.

Upon a rough stone table in the centre of the room was piled a
great heap of treasure and round it were grouped the remains of
three skeletons; a fourth man had evidently crawled some distance
towards the door before collapsing. As John knelt to examine the
fourth figure of tragedy he noticed a crumpled scrap of paper resting beneath the spread bones of the man's right hand. He lifted
the paper carefully.

"May the curse of all the gods fall upon Ram Das," he read, "for he has betrayed his salt and brought us to our death in the moment of triumph. May his limbs rot in agony in the desert he shall not cross, and may his soul wander in that desert until he shall being another of our race to reap the harvest of our labour."

The note was signed "Herbert Strangeways."

For a long moment John stood quite still, reading the writing over and over again, while the impression grew that he and Jubatalla were not alone. He turned at last to leave the cavern. By the door he seemed to see a dim figure, which salaamed deeply and departed, and yet Jubatalla saw no one, nor could they find any trace of footprints in the dust which lay deep upon the floor.

X
A MATTER OF MORALS

THERE IS, IN THE ADELPHI, LONDON, a queer society styling itself "The Discussion and Investigation Club." The membership comprises people of both sexes interested in unusual subjects, which they discuss and investigate with all due decency and decorum. Dabbling in the unusual is, however, a dangerous business, in the course of which polite draperies are sometimes torn aside, and the gruesome skeletons of grim realities unexpectedly become revealed.

To one meeting of this society came Alan Wright, big-game hunter by profession, instinct, and preference. How he drifted to the Adelphi, I know not. Perhaps a member invited him; perhaps he was given a letter of introduction to the secretary. In any case, it does not really matter. The main point is that he was there, and that the discussion on that particular occasion concerned the "Morality of Suicide."

Old Hunter Wright, who had been too long in the wilds to care much for the luxurious lounges and divans of civilisation, sat on a straight-backed chair in a corner of the room, puffing placidly at a big pipe, the biting smoke from which made the women in his immediate vicinity cough violently.

He looked an incongruous object in that smart assembly, clad as he was in an old brown shooting jacket, the pockets of which had long since bulged out of all shape from the weight of cartridges, and a low, yellow flannel collar, which was all in one piece with his shirt. His massive head was inclined slightly as he listened to the flow of polite platitudes and shallow opinions; his great golden beard gave him something of the appearance of a fierce old lion, and his eyes were extraordinarily steady—they did not blink, and were never moved from the face of the person speaking. This trick of steady gazing is a peculiar attribute of the outland man.

Mrs. Watson, the wife of a Cabinet Minister, who held pronounced views upon woman's suffrage, was speaking.

"I hold," she concluded, "that a woman is justified in taking her own life when there is no other means left to her of preserving her chastity."

As the lady resumed her seat a young clergyman of ascetic appearance rose.

"I am sorry," he said, "to have to disagree with Mrs. Watson, but I must maintain that life is the gift of God—a sacred trust imposed upon us by our Maker—and the self-infliction of death is tantamount to the refusal of His gift, and, as such, is the sin unpardonable, not to be justified by any set of circumstances. I have heard it said that sometimes God imposes conditions which clearly indicate His wish for the self-surrender of life, but this I do not believe. Life is to me a sacred trust, to be accounted for. Circumstances which may affect it adversely, or even make it seem to be unbearable, are, in my opinion, but a stricter testing of our stewardship."

Hunter Wright removed his pipe from his mouth, and leaned forward without rising.

"Excuse me speaking," he said, "but I once knew a lady who held similar opinions—with disastrous results. I may add that I do not agree with you at all!"

There was a pause, in which the twenty people in the room turned curiously towards the old hunter.

"Mr. Wright is a traveler and hunter of great experience," said the president, after a while. "He has doubtless seen many strange things in his wanderings, and his opinions we should, I am sure, be most interested to hear."

The hunter, who seemed suddenly to realise that he had spoken, looked bashfully at the reeking bowl of the big pipe he held in his hand, and which he now thrust hastily into his pocket.

"I'm afraid I'm a poor hand at giving opinions or setting out arguments," he said; "but I'll tell you the story, if you like, and then you must judge for yourselves."

There was a mingled murmur of polite interest and assent.

"A good many years ago," began the hunter, "when Africa was a deal more dangerous and mysterious than it is today, I was engaged by a gentleman, fresh out from home, to go with him in search of the 'Elephants' Graveyard.'

"Every African hunter knows the legend, which says that the elephants, who are alleged to know when they are going to die, travel almost incredible distances to the place where their forefathers died and where there is, therefore, a vast quantity of ivory.

"Despite the fact that the story is so well known in Africa, I was none the less surprised that my employer, Richard Barrett, should be so entirely conversant with it. But he told me that an uncle of his had been after the 'white stuff' years before, and he even produced a rough sketch map of the route we were to follow. You may be sure that I studied that map long and carefully. I opened my eyes at it, too, for it located the 'Grave Yard' in territory which was at that time totally unexplored. All we knew about it was that a small mission station had been established on the banks of a river which flowed through the unknown land, and that down that river came sinister rumours of savage tribes who were unfriendly to white people, and who feared only the Arab slave traders who raided them periodically.

"When I finished studying that map I began to realise that I was in for a bigger thing than I'd anticipated. Still, my word had been given, the pay was good, and I wasn't going back on the one, nor did I want to forfeit the other. But I didn't altogether fancy our chances of ever seeing civilisation again. On the other hand, if we did get back, we should be millionaires two or three times over, and that counted for a lot with me in those days.

"I'm not going to weary you with a long description of our journey up to the mission station, for it's the sort of record you can read in any book of travel.

"A surprise awaited us when we reached our pushing-off place for the Unknown, for I think that the last thing that either of us expected was to find a white woman in that perilous region, and I shall always maintain that it was criminal folly for the missionary, Mr. Wendover, to have taken his daughter, Stella, into those God-forgotten wilds.

"'Star,' she told me her name meant, and like a star she was; white, pure, and beautiful, and infinitely far from the human touch. She was tall and slim, with wavy, fair hair, dark eyebrows, and deep, dark eyes which were like forest pools in their mysteriousness. She was just twenty, and had been out from home less than a month, and so still retained a ruddy fairness of complexion which is peculiar to some women of Saxon origin. We stayed at the mission a month, getting together canoes and our *safari* of porters for the journey up the river and into the interior.

"I could see the way things were shaping, Dick Barrett and Stella were inseparable after the first twenty-four hours. It was a clear case of love at first sight. Long before dawn he'd be up and out of the hut, away into the bush to gather the big, white bell-blossoms she liked. If a lion roared in the night or a leopard called he'd jump for his rifle and rush out to prowl around the station until dawn came and relieved his mind of anxiety.

"One day, when I was sitting smoking with Mr. Wendover, I broached the subject of his daughter, pointing out to him the horrible dangers she ran from fever, snakes, and wild beasts, and, worst of all, from the slave-traders and savage natives.

"'My friend,' he said quietly, 'we are all vessels in the hands of God, to break or preserve as He deems best.'

"Somehow his sublime faith made me angry, and I told him pretty sharply that that might be as he said, but, anyway, he should make his daughter carry a revolver, and teach her to keep the last bullet for herself in case of need; for I'd had some experience of the slave traders' ways.

"Curiously enough, the advice, which I still consider perfectly sound, seemed to annoy him.

"'Hunter Wright,' he replied, indignantly. 'Stella might well carry a weapon, but she would keep no bullet for such a coward's purpose, for she believes, as I do, that self-murder is the sin unthinkable.'

"I saw that it was no use arguing with him and so the matter dropped.

"The night before we started on the second stage of our journey Barrett came back to the hut very late. There was a firm set about his big shoulders as he lowered his long limbs on to his bed, but his eyes were sad and troubled.

"'Alan,' he said to me, 'we've got to get that ivory somehow. All my money is in this venture. Not that that matters much, but I shall want money when we get back, because Stella and I are going to be married. I'm horribly worried about Stella, and I've been asking her father to send her home, but he won't hear of it, says it would be like doubting the goodness of his God.'

"I said something about doing our best and trusting to luck, and then we went to sleep. Next morning we started at daybreak. Stella and her father waved their handkerchiefs to us until our canoes bore us out of sight around a bend in the river.

"We were more than a year cut off from civilisation, searching for the ivory, and then we found it. My God! Shall I ever forget that day? We had been pushing steadily on through dense bush since early morning, and were just thinking of halting for our midday meal when we struck a hard-beaten road, as broad as Piccadilly. I stared and stared for I could hardly believe the evidence of my eyes, but there it was, stretching away and away, straight and wide between the boles of the forest trees.

"'*Njia ya Tembo!*' ('The Road of the Elephants') exclaimed an old native hunter, standing at my elbow, and then I knew that we had found what no other white man had ever seen, the Elephants' Road, stamped flat by the feet of countless generations, to the Elephants' Grave Yard.

"We followed that road, which led, straight and true, mile upon mile, until it ended suddenly at the edge of a terrific precipice.

"Throwing down our loads we lay flat upon the ground, and craned our necks out over the brink. There, hundreds of feet below us, we saw a great mass of bones gleaming redly in the last rays of the setting sun. But, as we looked and our eyes became accustomed to the depth of the pit, we were able to descry the smoother flash of ivory among the heaped-up bones.

"Ivory! Do I say ivory! There was more ivory in that pit than man has ever dreamed of. It is the storehouse of the world. And it is cursed, every tusk of it.

"For a month we toiled, raising the 'white stuff' from the depths by ropes and improvised pulleys, until we had as much as our two hundred porters could carry, every man overburdened, and making no more than ten miles a day, whereas with sixty-pound loads they would have done thirty, and we could have been back in half the time for more, but the lust of wealth was on us and we would not leave a single ounce we could carry away.

"After four months we came to a river village where we were able to get canoes in which to paddle down to the mission.

"When we got there the place was a mass of smoking ruins. As we prodded about among the debris we heard a feeble voice calling to us, and heaving aside the smoking remains of a big hut we discovered Mr. Wendover, the missionary, *in extremis*. Some instinct must have led him to anticipate our coming, otherwise I do not think he could have lasted so long, for he was ripped open and half burned alive.

"'Stella!' he gasped, 'the Arabs—have taken—her—away!'

"The broken sentence was torn from his lips and every word was followed by a gush of bright blood. For awhile he lay still with his head upon my arm and then we got the story from him word by painful word.

"Yesterday the Arabs had passed with a big convoy of slaves under the yoke, and he had gone out to remonstrate with them. Then they had attacked the mission, putting all to the spear, except a few of the younger women and Stella, whom he had seen driven off under the cruel hippopotamus hide whips, yoked neck to neck with one of his few converts.

"He told the tale as one who had held himself back from death to fulfil a trust, and then he died quietly, and apparently unconscious of the fearful tragedy which had befallen.

"When I had laid him down I met Dick's eyes, and I hope that I may never again see such an expression as informed them. They were the eyes of a soul damned and in torment.

"'We have come twenty-four hours too late. My God, too late!' he whispered, and, turning, walked away to where our tents were being pitched. Before I saw him again I had buried all that remained of Christopher Wendover.

Later, when I went to the tent we shared, I found Dick sitting on the edge of his bed staring in front of him with unseeing eyes. For awhile I busied myself with the arrangement of my kit. Presently he became aware of me.

"'Alan,' he said, 'tell the boy to bring food. We shall need all our strength. Tomorrow I start to find Stella.'

"'To-morrow we start,' I corrected him.

"'You will go with me, old fellow?' he said, reaching out for my hand. 'I hoped you would.'

"Soon after dawn next morning we paid off our porters and moved north again, taking with us only our gun bearers, personal boys, and a dozen *wapazazi* to carry our kit.

"For six months we traveled up and down the unexplored lands seeking news. One village after another, that the Arabs had passed through, we visited, hearing always the same news of the white woman who had marched with them.

"At last we heard fresh tidings. The white woman had been sold to a native chief, who had taken her still further into the unknown bush, whither he was returning to his village from a successful raid. Him we found, but the chief had no white woman in his village and professed never to have bought one.

"By this time our money was exhausted. We had not enough even to pay our servants. We went back to civilisation and sold our ivory before returning to the bush to resume our search. But the trail was blurred. Hither and thither we journeyed, following one false rumour after another. Twice we came across white women who were no more than half-castes, and at each fresh failure Dick only set his jaw more squarely and grew the more determined to carry on the search, for the rest of his natural life if need be.

"In those days I learned to love the man for his splendid purpose and the unbroken resolution which seemed never to fail him. Once I suggested to him that long ere this Stella Wendover would have finished the pitiful tragedy by her own hand.

"'No,' he said, 'you did not know her as I did, she would never do that.'

"After nearly two years had passed we gathered what seemed certain news of her from a wandering native, who said that the chief who had bought her from the Arabs had sold her again to his paramount chief still further in the interior.

"We took up the search with renewed hope, although, for my part, I could not see what was to be the outcome of it all, even if we should find her in the end.

"From the last point of civilisation we marched at the head of a *safari* of a hundred porters bearing our stores, and plenty of such 'trade goods' as the natives were only too anxious to acquire in those days.

"After months of marching through heartbreaking country we reached a big native town where I do not believe any white man had ever been seen before. At any rate, the whole population turned out and stared curiously at us.

"The king kept us waiting twenty-four hours before he would see us, and then received us in state. He was the most repulsive savage I have ever seen, despite the magnificent head-dress of ostrich plumes and the leopard skin cloak he wore. He was jet black, his bulk enormous, and his little pig-like eyes glistened above fat, flabby cheeks. He did not rise to meet us, but sat sullenly upon an ebony-wood stool in the midst of his councilors.

"We explained to him our mission through the medium of an interpreter. He admitted a white woman was there, but, at first, said she was not for sale; the sight of our trade goods, however, made him change his mind. Presently the white slave was sent for. After we had waited upwards of an hour I asked the interpreter the cause of the delay.

"'The *bibi* is attiring herself suitably,' he said.

"I think that we both expected to see a white woman appear in civilised garments. The shock was therefore all the greater when presently a girl approached the king clad only in a grass skirt and sundry jingling anklets. Her body was so sunbronzed that for the moment I doubted if she was anything more than a particularly light-coloured native. I had, moreover, looked for a fair-haired woman, but this one's hair was stiffened with red clay and dressed native fashion. She passed us with head averted, but turned to face us at the king's command.

"I heard Dick catch a little sobbing breath and thrust out my hand to steady him, but he pushed it aside.

"As she turned slowly round I felt the sweat start out all over my body. Then I wished to God that I was anywhere but where I was, for the woman staring at us with steady eyes was a living horror. A broad, flat piece of bone was thrust through the lower lip, completely destroying the shape of the mouth, upon the cheeks great scars had been burned deep by the juice of the candelabra euphorbia plant, and round the eyes were tattooed many circles of tiny cuts, into which wood-ash had been rubbed.

"But it was the woman's eyes which shocked me most, they held no light of recognition, only the infinite patience of a dog that has been many times beaten.

"What Dick suffered in those moments I can only imagine by my own feelings. But we were not done with horrors yet, for as the woman turned away again the shape of her figure made plain her condition.

"I looked from her to Dick. His face was like the mask of a dead man.

"'My God! Alan,' he muttered, 'Who is she? She's white, but she can't be Stella.'

"'Speak to her, man,' I said, 'if she is Stella, the sound of your voice may rouse her memory.'

"He took a step forward and touched the woman fearfully upon the arm.

"'If you are Stella,' he said, 'for pity's sake speak to me.'

She looked straight into his eyes without any sign of recognition. When he spoke to her again she turned to the interpreter, saying something in the guttural native dialect.

"'What does she say?' asked Dick.

"'She asks, Master, who you are and what you want with her,' the interpreter replied.

"'Tell her,' said Dick, 'she need fear nothing, I am of her people, and, whether she is she whom I seek or another, I will buy her from the king and take her back to her own land.'

"When this speech was translated the woman flung herself down upon the ground, groveling at the king's feet, pawing his obese body and hiding her face against his knees.

"At first he seemed impervious to her pleadings. She sprang to her feet and pointed to her figure. At that he seemed to reflect for a moment.

"'Tell the white men,' he said to the interpreter, 'they shall have the woman, but not until my son has been born.'

"Dick offered to buy the child as well, but to that the king would not agree. Apparently he was in need of an heir to his throne.

"We went back to the hut that had been allotted to us, and talked things over. We were quite convinced the woman was not Stella, but, as Dick had said, she was white, and it was up to us to get her out of that hell, with her consent or without it. Dick would touch no food, and after awhile we lay down and slept.

"In the night I was awakened by the sound of the grass mat being stealthily pulled aside from the door. By the faint light of the lamp I saw the white woman creep furtively in. I lay still, breathing regularly as if asleep, and watched her through half-closed lids. After one glance in my direction she crossed the hut and stood looking down at Dick while the big tears coursed fast down her seared cheeks. After what seemed a long time she knelt down and touched him with soft caressing hands. Then she left the hut as silently as she had entered it.

"Before I had made up my mind what to do the dawn came and Dick awakened. A moment later an uproar arose in the town. Presently the interpreter rushed into the hut.

"'The white woman is dead,' he cried. 'She has killed herself.'

"Then, like a fool, I blurted out what I had witnessed in the night.

"'I see,' said Dick quietly, 'she would not die to save herself, but has died now to save me suffering. She thought that I should never know.'

"He walked outside, and a moment later I heard the sharp report of a revolver. When I got to him he was quite dead, for the merciful bullet had scattered his brains."

* * * * * *

When the old hunter stopped speaking, absolute silence was maintained in the big room.

"That is all the story, ladies and gentlemen," he said at last.

"But I think that Stella Wendover would have been justified in taking her life when the Arabs first attacked the mission, for she was a refined, religious, English gentlewoman, and her subsequent sufferings, both mental and physical, must have been well nigh beyond bearing. And I would have you remember that she did not kill herself until she knew that Dick Barrett intended to take her back to civilisation, when her identity must become known sooner or later and his mental agony would have come to equal her own."

The members of the "Discussion and Investigation Club" said nothing. Only the convulsive sobbing of the Honourable Charlotte Watson broke the silence as the old hunter got to his feet and left the room.

XI
ACCORDING TO THE LAW

I

HALF A DOZEN MEN were sitting in the back room of Benjamin's bar in Johannesburg, wishing that something would turn up. They had finished playing poker a couple of hours ago, the remittance man's last instalment from "home" being by that time completely exhausted.

A native "boy" had just brought in the eighth instalment of whisky and water. The little room was so thick with smoke and so acrid with the pungent fumes of Boer tobacco that the average man would not have been able either to see or breathe. To the six inmates of the room the foul and fuggy atmosphere seemed to make no difference at all.

The doctor had finished a long yarn about the killing of a big sable antelope and a subsequent startling adventure with vultures when his hunting partner had left him to guard the carcass against their depredations.

"I was pretty green in those days," he concluded, "and I shall always think that Schmidt knew the danger and left me to it as a means of paying off a grudge he held against me for a little plain speaking I had been forced to earlier in the day as to his right to the use of my personal belongings."

An old prospector leaned forward across the table, spreading his sinewy arms carefully amongst the glasses, and stared through the smoke in the doctor's direction.

The prospector was not prepossessing. He was a man of over sixty years of age, whose countenance the African sun had scorched and dried to the yellowness of old parchment. His chin and cheeks were thatched with a straggling growth of iron-grey hair, a big soft hat flopped untidily over his eyes. The ragged shirt he wore was glazed with dirt; the sleeves, rolled back to the elbows, disclosed arms extraordinarily well formed and muscular for a man of his age.

"What was Schmidt, a back-veldt Boer?" he queried.

In answer to the doctor's affirmation, the prospector laughed softly. A peculiarly mirthless laugh.

"I thought so," he said; "they're all the same—dirty white, with a yellow streak. Some of the things that go on on those back-veldt farms would turn a Kaffir sick and send a white man with any morals mad. But I'll say this for them, they're good haters!"

"Hate," said the remittance man softly, "and the yellow streak! They are not confined entirely to the Boers, I fancy!"

The bank manager coughed discreetly, for he knew the story of Wainwright, who had just spoken.

"I have often thought," continued Wainwright, "that the smallest causes for offence breed the biggest enmities."

"I don't agree with you there," said the doctor. "A man must have a pretty good cause for offence before he works up what I should call a real 'killing hate.' Of course, with the Latin races it is different. They are so infernally touchy and excitable that one can never tell how to deal with them. Look at their absurd vendettas, for example. A man treads accidentally on another man's toes, or jostles him in a crowd and their descendants, for untold generations, magnify the incident into cause for an unending blood-feud."

"But surely the same state of things appertains in England in a less dangerous degree," interposed the bank manager. "Otherwise, how do you account for those extraordinary lawsuits, in the long course of which a prosperous man will beggar himself for the sake of an unimportant right of way?"

"Law!" said the old prospector, spitting contemptuously; "law! I don't think much of your civilised law that sends a poor devil of a starving woman to gaol for stealing a loaf of bread, and yet lets one of these damned, nigger-driving, gold-grubbing company promoters who have ruined Africa, skin widows and half-witted clergymen bare of every bean they possess without punishment."

"But, my friend," replied the bank manager, "laws are made by civilised peoples for the greater comfort of the whole community; without them society could no longer exist."

"And you think that laws which are so involved as to leave plenty of loopholes for clever thieves, wife-stealers, and murderers to slip through are good laws, do you?" asked the prospector bitterly. "I tell you," he went on, banging his fist down so violently that the glasses leapt again on the table, "that there is no law in the world so just as the law of the wild. 'First blood-hunter's meat.' What could be fairer than that? For it saves all after-dispute as to who fired the fatal shot. In the wilds we are governed by Nature. We kill the man who carries off our woman, and we wipe out a deadly insult in blood. Primitive law, if you like, but it's Bible law none the less. 'An eye for an eye, a tooth for a tooth, and a life for a life.' Can you dispute the justice of it?"

A long silence followed this apparently irrefutable contention, and it seemed that a fruitful source of argument must lie fallow for want of further material upon which to feed.

Suddenly Benjamin, the bar-keeper, pushed open the door and shuffled forward to the table.

"Red Jake's dead," he said, and paused expectantly for the rain of questions he knew must follow, for a death always excites interest in any community. In this particular case only Benjamin and the old prospector, Jim Lyall, had been long enough in the country to remember the wild days which had provided an adequate setting for Red Jake's hectic career.

"How'd it happen?" asked the prospector, fanning the smoke away from his face.

"An old native named Umpomba went out with Jake hunting lion and got him with an assegai while he was asleep. The mounted police have just brought the 'boy' in. You remember him, Jim. He was the fellow who gave evidence against Jake at the trial, and after it was over swore that he'd revenge his sister, if he waited a lifetime. Well, he's waited thirty years and now he's done it."

"There you are," said Lyall to the company at large, "there are two cases of hate which ought to settle your arguments."

"What's the story, Jim?" asked the doctor. "I've heard of this man Red Jake as a dangerous character, and knew that he was tried for murder a good many years ago, but it was so long before my time that I never heard any details of the case."

"Well, it's a pretty complicated tale," said Lyall, "but I'll do my best to tell it, unless Benjamin here would rather spin the yarn?"

"Not me," said Benjamin hastily, "I'm no good at talking; besides, I've got to keep my eye on the bar, but I'll stay and listen for old times' sake."

"Things weren't as orderly out here in the early nineties as they are now," Lyall commenced. "Southern Rhodesia was the frontier, as far as South Africa was concerned, and Fort Victoria was the first settlement founded in Mashonaland by the Pioneer Column of the Chartered Company. Speaking generally, it was a quiet, well-ordered little settlement, but on Saturday nights things were apt to get a bit complicated.

"Most days if you wandered into the main street you'd find a dog making things unpleasant for his insect friends, and maybe a couple of native women taking snuff outside the little store; the Company's maps showed a township of six streets, seven avenues, a market square, a church, and a museum; as a matter of fact, there was one street, comprising four or five shanties and some tin-roofed buildings, running from the Drift to the 'Thatched House.' The market square was a ragged patch beside the hotel. The church and museum didn't exist.

"Some men had offices, which they used mostly as lumber rooms; if they wanted to do business they went to the 'Thatched House,' which was our one hotel, where everybody fed and where the whole life of the town centred.

"In Victoria we did everything collectively, from celebrating a birthday to burying a member of the community.

"Under these circumstances you may be sure we were none too pleased when Red Jake arrived and ran up a shack for himself just outside the town. He was neither congenial nor desirable; in fact, he was a 'mean white' of the worst order. He was a holy terror to the natives and soon began to terrorise the white population as well.

"He was a great big bulky brute six feet two high, as thick as an oak-tree and as strong as an ox. He would stamp into the 'Thatched House,' order drinks round and stop all business and gambling while he was there. After two or three drinks he'd get most infernally offensive. We all tackled him in turn, but he just made mincemeat of us, which is saying a lot, for we were a pretty hard-bitten crowd.

"After this state of things had lasted best part of two months, a youngster turned up fresh from home, with an unspoiled complexion, and the red of sappy British beef still showing in his cheeks. I fancy he'd got into some sort of bother at one of the universities and had been sent abroad to save trouble. He was a fine, cleanly-built lad, though not over big. His name was Mercer. He seemed to realise that he was new to our life, and would learn most from the overseas men by keeping a still tongue in his head and not asserting himself. Red Jake was away when he arrived and did not turn up until he'd been settled in best part of a month.

"One night, when I was standing by the bar talking to Mercer, Red Jake swaggered in.

"'Drinks on me,' he shouts, then he catches sight of Mercer. 'Who the hell are you?' he asks.

"'My name's Mercer,' the boy replied.

"'Oh, it is, is it!' says Jake; then, turning to the barman, he adds: 'Bring a bottle for the baby, Joe.'

"'Ain't got no bottles, Jake,' says Joe nervously.

"'Then bring him a glass of milk,' Jake answers.

"'I don't think I particularly want to drink with you,' chips in young Mercer, looking his man up and down. At that Jake flushes up and turns to Joe.

"'Bring that milk and be damn sharp about it,' he orders.

"When it was brought he goes up close to Mercer.

"'Are you going to drink this?' he says.

"'No!' answers the boy.

"'Then I'll wash your face with it,' says Jake, and with that he chucks the lot smack into Mercer's face.

"Mercer didn't hesitate a minute. He hit out like a kicking mule and Jake went down with a crash. I was mighty sorry for the boy, for I'd seen Jake fight, but I might have saved my sympathy.

"Jake got up and the 'Thatched House' emptied into the street quicker'n hell, for we wanted to see the fight.

"Jake was in his shirt sleeves and didn't need to peel. Young Mercer stripped off his coat and shirt, too, and chucked them to me to hold. It was then we began to wonder if he'd got a sporting chance after all, for he stripped like a fighting man. His head was well set on and his chest deeper than we had imagined. He was thin on the flanks, but his arm and shoulder muscles were what amazed us, for they rolled and rippled like steel springs under the smooth white flesh, which had not yet been tanned by the African sun. Jake seemed to realise something of the same sort, for I saw him eyeing his opponent critically.

"I wish I could do that fight justice, for it was the most beautiful exhibition of brains and skill against brute force I've ever seen.

"Jake stood square on his huge legs. He looked like a monument and you couldn't imagine him being knocked down. We knew from past experience that, despite his weight, he could move quick enough when he wanted.

"He bulked so much bigger than his opponent, however, and his massive, ugly face looked so menacing that I for one began to fear afresh for young Mercer. He, for his part, did not seem in the least anxious. Stripped to the waist, he stepped forward ready and looked towards the sergeant of police, who, for formalities' sake, held a watch in the palm of his hand.

"'Time!' called the sergeant.

"Mercer faced his man with little weaving intricate steps, breaking to left and right in a way which bespoke a previous knowledge of ringcraft. He was feeling his way, while Jake, with a watchful eye, pivoted slowly upon his right leg, his left arm partly extended, his right held low to guard the mark. This was different to his usual mad-bull, overbearing rush and showed that he appreciated something of his opponent's value. Suddenly he rushed in, hitting with all his might, but each time Mercer was just beyond the range of the great fists, watching his man and waiting for an opening. Almost immediately after he led lightly with his left and then led again, getting home each time, but there seemed to be no power behind the blows. Then it was 'time.' Mercer was quite fresh, but Jake's great hairy chest was labouring stormily.

"Jake opened the second round with a sudden rush, but Mercer slipped sideways and avoided him, then sprang in and delivered a stinging punch to the ribs, which set Jake gasping for breath; elated by his slight success, the boy led for the face, but got a swinging counter to the jaw which shook him sadly. Instantly Jake rushed in to complete his work, but Mercer, with his better knowledge of the art, kept out of harm's way until the end of the round.

"As the boy rested upon my knee I offered him a sip from my flask, but he waved it away.

"'I may need it later,' he said.

"He was on his feet in a flash at the call of 'time.' He went straight for his man, his fists getting home with two clean smacks, one to the ribs, the other flush between the eyes. That second punch would have fetched most men off their feet, but it did no more than daze Jake for a second. Mercer must have felt that he was winning then, for he mixed it up proper, but he got into a clinch with Jake which was nearly the end of him, for the big man smashed in a terrible uppercut which the boy only half broke with his guard. Jake tried another. Mercer dodged it, but got a swinging blow on the ear as he broke away. Then it was 'time' again. He came back to me with a bloody head, but still quite fit and able to take a lot more punishment.

"For a couple of rounds more they fought guardedly, feeling for openings and not finding them. Jake's hitting was the harder, but the boy was the quicker upon his feet. He had learned a lesson, too, and so kept out of another clinch. There was no cheering in those rounds; nothing but the quick patter of the men's feet, the soft thud of blows and the hissing intake of laboured breath.

"In the eighth round Mercer seemed to see an opening, for he sprang in swift as a leopard. There was a crack like a pistol shot, his head flew back, his arms whirled wide and there he was on his back in the road, with his neck well-nigh broken. Jake stepped forward with his right held ready, but half a dozen men dragged him back as the police-sergeant began to count. At the count of 'five' Mercer struggled to his knees, at 'seven' he was on his feet. Jake rushed in, but the boy stumbled to the side again and yet again, instinctively keeping clear of those sledge-hammer fists until the end of the round.

"He sagged heavy on my knee that time as I fanned him with my old big-brimmed hat. Just before the minute was up he snatched the flask from my hand and drained it. Jake saw the action and grinned, but he did not feel the boy's body thrill and stiffen to the raw spirit as I did. For two minutes they sparred cautiously. Then Jake tried one of his mad rushes. That cost him the fight, for Mercer had been waiting for this. As Jake closed in the boy's fist shot out with all the weight of his body behind it. It was a beautiful blow, fair to the point of the scrubby, unshaven chin. Jake went down like a felled tree the axe-men have wedged. He lay on his back with his arms thrown wide and his limbs twitching. He struggled spasmodically once or twice, but he could not manage to rise and the sergeant counted him out in proper Queensberry style.

"God, how we cheered! There was that great hulking bully who had terrorised us all, beaten by a boy barely out of his 'teens,' who he himself had called 'baby' not an hour ago.

"After that Jake went away. He was living pretty intricate with a native woman named Usta at the time and took her with him. Before he went he came into the 'Thatched House' with his face all patched up and swore that he'd have Mercer's life before he'd finished, for, as I've said, he was a 'mean white,' and couldn't take his licking like a man, although he'd brought the trouble on himself.

"Shortly afterwards Mercer took a farm eighty miles up country, after which we didn't see him more than about once in three months, when he came in for supplies or to do business.

"Months went by and we didn't see anything more of Red Jake. But he hadn't forgotten; he was only biding his time and waiting an opportunity to take his revenge.

"One night when we were all sitting in the 'Thatched House' playing a game of Whisky-Poker, which had been in progress best part of five weeks, we heard the beat of horse's hoofs coming up the street from the Drift. I wasn't playing at the time, so went outside to see who it was. I got a pretty big surprise when I saw young Mercer roped and riding between two mounted policemen.

"I asked what was the matter and he told me he was under arrest on a charge of murdering a native woman. I asked the corporal of the escort for some further particulars, but he could only tell me that a man named Jake Jubert had laid an information at the police post that a native woman had been burned to death by Mercer on his farm and that the informer had gone off saying he would be back in a few days' time to give evidence before the magistrate if they caught Mercer.

"'Red Jake,' thinks I to myself. 'This is the beginning of his revenge.'

"Next morning I went to see Mercer, who was locked up in a shed adjoining the Fort. He told me that he had been away hunting when the woman—who was not one of his people—had been done to death. He added that he had been on his way to inform the authorities of the matter when he had met the corporal and trooper of police who had arrested him.

"I knew that the Assizes were not for another two months, so that morning I dug out for Mercer's place to find out what had happened.

"All the 'boys' were very frightened and at first would say nothing, but I did not need to bother, for Mercer's Hottentot hunter, 'Mustard,' had already got the story pieced together. I knew that I could rely upon his word, for he was mighty fond of his master, was 'Mustard.'

"'*Baas*,' he said, 'the "boys" are afraid to tell the truth because of the Red *Baas*, who came here after we had gone hunting, but me they have told all that they saw and all that they heard from the Red *Baas's* "boys."'

"'Well, and what have they told you?' I asked.

"'Do you remember the woman, Usta, who went away with the Red *Baas* after my *baas* had beaten him?' he asked, by way of reply.

"I told him 'Yes.'

"'Well,' said he, 'he caught her trying to run away with one of his *voorlopers*, and told her she should suffer for it; then he brought her here while we were away and shut her up in one of our huts. That night he set fire to the hut and burned her to death. Next morning he beat the farm "boys" with the sjambok and told them if they did not say that my *baas* had burned the woman he would come back and beat them to death.'

"I got this story corroborated by the farm 'boys' and also collected the evidence of the 'boys' who had been away hunting with Mercer. Then I rode back to Victoria and saw the magistrate. He listened to what 'Mustard' and I had to say, and after that he ordered Mercer to be released.

"I met him when he came out, and I never saw a man so angry in my life.

"'The dirty white-livered swine!' he raged. 'To think that after being beaten in a fair fight, brought about by a quarrel of his own seeking, he should try to get back at me this way. Think of it! He burned that woman out of sheer devilry and then tried to fix the murder on to me. I know that after the fight he swore to have my blood, but I thought at the time that that was only his evil temper speaking. In any case I should have expected that he'd try to get me at the risk of his own dirty hide.'

"The next day a police patrol was ordered out to hunt for Jake on a charge of murder. When the news reached us Mercer went straight to the Fort and asked the police officer in charge for permission to join in the hunt, but the official wouldn't hear of it.

"Mercer came back to me cursing like a stevedore. Nothing would content him but he must set off on a private man-hunt of his own. I tried my best to dissuade him, but his mind was quite made up. Seeing the sort of temper he was in, I decided to go along, too, to make sure that he didn't get arrested on a second, and better-founded, charge of murder. There was a nasty, purposeful look in his eye that boded ill for Red Jake if we found him.

"Just as we were starting out a fine big Zulu, who had been squatting on his heels in the road, got up and stalked majestically over to where we were standing beside the horses.

"He gave the usual form of greeting, then stood silent, waiting for one of us to speak. He was magnificently built, even for a Zulu. He looked like a big bronze statue, standing upright in the sun-glare.

"'Well, what do you want?' I asked.

"'*Baas!*' he said, addressing Mercer, 'you go to seek the Slaughterer.' '*Bulalio*' was the word he used.

"'What is that to you?' Mercer asked.

"'Because, *baas*, I am Umpomba, brother of Usta, whom *Bulalio* burned to death at your kraal.'

"'A valuable ally,' said Mercer, turning to me and speaking in English. 'What do you think?'

"'Take him by all means,' I replied. 'He will find out far more than we can hope to do of where Red Jake is in hiding.'

"So Umpomba came with us. After we had been trekking best part of a week he brought us the first definite news of the man we were after. Up to that time we had followed his trail by guesswork and hearsay.

"'*Baas*,' said Umpomba, coming up to our camp-fire one night, 'I have found *Bulalio* and have watched his hiding-place all through the heat of the day.'

"'Where is he, then?' asked Mercer eagerly.

"'Not ten miles from here,' came the unexpected answer, 'there is a kloof in the hills, by the big mountains. It is deep and very narrow at the entering in, so that half-a-dozen determined men might hold it easily against an *impi*. And,' he added, after a pause during which he took snuff, '*Bulalio* has five other white men and some "bad" natives with him now.'

"This information fairly staggered us, for we had expected to find our quarry alone with a few native servants.

"We stayed where we were among the kopjes for awhile after that. Umpomba used to go out every morning before dawn and lay up in hiding during the day, watching the mouth of the kloof where Red Jake and his friends were concealed. They didn't seem in a hurry to move on. That suited us very well, for we couldn't tackle the lot single-handed and so had sent a 'boy' back with a note to the police officer at Fort Victoria. We expected the police to arrive any time within a fortnight.

"On the tenth day, when we were lying on our backs in the shade of a big ant-heap, smoking our after-breakfast pipes, we heard someone approaching. We sat up, and saw old Umpomba—or rather 'young' Umpomba as he was then—running towards us on swift-moving feet, as strong and nearly as fleet as those of a buck.

"'*Baas*,' he cried, as soon as he was within speaking distance, 'they have all gone except *Bulalio*, and he is only waiting to see the last of the gear packed.'

"We jumped to our feet and ran quickly back to camp, shouting to the 'boys' to saddle the horses. In less than five minutes' we were galloping hell for leather across the veldt, Umpomba hanging on to my stirrup-leather and running with long, untiring strides.

"We dismounted about fifty yards from the kloof, approached quietly and, seeing no one, went in with a rush through the narrow opening. Red Jake heard us coming and, throwing up his revolver, fired twice as we came into view. I heard Umpomba gasp, turned my head as I ran and saw him down on the ground with the blood spurting from a hole in his thigh. We were on to Jake before he could fire again. All three of us went down in a tearing, fighting, scratching, cursing bunch. Then another man, whom Umpomba evidently had overlooked, must have run out from one of the huts, for I got a kick in the ribs that made me fairly gasp. I rolled clear of Mercer and Jake and sprang to my feet, to face this new antagonist. He was a short, thick-set fellow, strongly-built and with terribly long arms. He held a knife in his right hand, but, luckily for me, had forgotten his gun in his anxiety to see what all the row was about.

"He came at me with a rush, but I'd dealt with knife-armed *dagoes* before. As he threw back his arm to strike I kicked upwards with all my strength and caught him fairly on the elbow with the toe of my boot, so that the knife flew from his paralysed fingers.

"Then we closed.

"Gad! but that was a fight. This way and that we tugged and struggled, but neither of us could make much headway against the other, though both were wishful, and all the time I could hear Mercer and Red Jake snarling, swearing and striving on the ground near my feet. I felt the sweat soaking through my clothing and running down from under my hat into my eyes.

"We should have stood there and struggled till the Day of Judgment, I believe, if my foot hadn't hit against a stone. I felt it turn under my boot, and down I went, with my opponent on top of me. As we lay there hugging each other, he suddenly loosed his hold and reached out over my shoulder; next time I saw his hand it held the rock that had tripped me. He held it high for a second, then bashed it down on to the side of my head.

"I didn't know anything else after that till I woke up to find Mercer splashing water in my face. Jake, looking pretty sick and shaky, was roped to a tree close by. Umpomba, who had managed to crawl up, was covering the hole in his leg with one hand, and over-aweing the natives with Mercer's revolver, which he held in the other. Mercer didn't mean letting those 'boys' go; he wanted them as evidence at Red Jake's trial.

"As soon as I was fit to sit up Mercer went off and fetched the horses. I rode one and Umpomba the other. Mercer drove the herd of frightened natives before him with his revolver held ready. Jake was roped to my stirrup.

"We didn't lose any time in lighting out, for we didn't want my antagonist, who had made good his escape, to find us there when he returned with his pals.

"A fortnight later we reached Victoria. There was a pretty big celebration in the 'Thatched House' that night, after Jake and his 'boys' were safely 'jugged.'"

II

The prospector paused and slowly refilled his big, deep-bowled Dutch pipe. Having lit it carefully he shut down the lid and puffed meditatively for a few minutes.

"What happened?" asked the remittance man. "Did he escape?"

"No!" said Lyall. "He didn't."

"Then why wasn't he hanged?" asked the doctor. "There seems to have been plenty of evidence."

"I'm going to tell you—when you've called for another round of drinks. This talking gives a man a worse thirst than the dust of the Kalahari Desert," said Lyall.

The doctor hastened to take the hint. When the drinks were brought the old prospector slowly drained his tumbler and heaved a sigh of satisfaction.

"Next morning," he continued, "Jake was brought before the magistrate, who committed him to the Assizes, due to be held a fortnight later.

"On the afternoon before the trial half a dozen strangers rode into the town. Rough-looking customers they were, but they didn't make any trouble and kept sober through the evening, which was more than we expected of them. In fact, their very quietness and moderation made me uneasy.

"Next morning the little room which did duty as a Court House was packed to suffocation. I saw the six strangers scattered amongst the crowd, and I remember thinking it funny that they had not stuck together; still they might have arrived separately or got split up in the crush. Two of them were posted on either side of the human alley through which the prisoner would be brought presently.

"The judge came in and took his seat. Then Red Jake was brought in. His face was sullen and hopeless as he passed through the door, but I saw his eyes light up as he looked round the crowded room. As the prisoner was led forward, it seemed to me, standing near, that one of the strangers leaned forward and dropped something into his pocket.

"It took best part of the morning to wade through the evidence, which was given mostly by natives.

"Jake's only defence was a complete denial of everything.

"Then the judge summed up. He pointed out the brutal nature of the crime, and the motive which had led up to it and which, he said, was one of double revenge, firstly, against the woman Usta for wishing to return to a man of her own colour, and, secondly, against Mercer on account of the fight in which the prisoner had been beaten. He drew attention to the deliberate manner in which the whole affair had been planned, even down to the laying of a false accusation against Mercer. Altogether it seemed a clear case of 'Jake for the long drop.'

"As the judge finished speaking I looked up and saw Umpomba with his head half through the window taking in every word, for he understood English well.

"The jury didn't need to retire to consider their finding. For a minute or two they conferred together in whispers. The foreman rose to his feet.

"'My lord—' he began, then stopped dead.

"You could have heard a pin drop in the Court House, for each of those six strangers was standing up with a brace of revolvers in his fists, and I had not been wrong about the stranger by the door dropping something into the prisoner's pocket, for Red Jake, too, had a gun in his hand.

"'See here,' he said, leaning forward and glaring fiercely at the foreman, 'you find me "Not guilty," else me an' my pals 'll blow pertikler hell outer this community!'

"The judge half rose from his chair, and Jake's pistol swung round instantly to cover him.

"'Sit down!' he snapped, and the judge sank back.

"Gad, but he was a brave man—that judge.

"'You will gain nothing by this show of armed force,' he said. 'I shall do my duty and pass sentence in accordance with the finding, whatever happens after.' Then he turned to the jury. 'Gentlemen,' he said, 'I'm waiting for your finding.'

"I saw the foreman look furtively around as if seeking a way of escape. Finding none, he hesitated a second longer, moistened his lips and looked appealingly at his fellow jurors.

"'Not guilty!' he stammered at last, flushing up to the roots of his sandy hair as the words left his lips.

"It was a day of unexpected happenings, but things weren't finished yet.

"Umpomba thrust his head and shoulders right in through the window.

"'White men,' he shouted, 'you would let go the Red Slaughterer who burned to death my sister Usta! Then, for Usta's sake, I swear by the *Inkoosizana-y-Zulu*—the Queen of the Heavens—to be revenged, aye, even if I have to wait a lifetime!'

"Then the strangers surged forward and surrounded Jake before they all backed out of the door together, the muzzles of their revolvers covering us the while.

"A moment later we heard the beat of their horses' hoofs upon the road, and immediately after that a mighty splashing as they dashed through the Drift."

* * * * * *

Lyall slowly scraped out the bowl of his pipe and spat contemplatively upon the floor.

"Jake hated for no reason at all," he said, "and failed to get his revenge. Old Umpomba was a good hater in a just cause, and has fulfilled his vow after waiting thirty years. But what always beat me was why Red Jake was never recaptured and hanged after a fresh trial."

"I can explain that," said the bank manager. "It is a point of English law—in force in Mashonaland in those days—that a man once tried for an offence and acquitted cannot be again tried for the same offence, not even though he publicly confesses his guilt."

"Ah!" said Lyall, the prospector, reflectively. "Civilised law's a rum thing. Personally I prefer the Law of the Wild. Old Umpomba's brand, for example!"

XII
RETRIBUTION

THERE WERE THREE CONSUMPTIVES, an inebriate, and a very malarious elephant hunter—all sent to sea by doctors' orders for the benefit of the health which it was hoped the salt sea breezes would blow into their deficient organisations.

The five, having been sent to sea expressly to be in the life-giving air, not unnaturally spent most of their time in the stuffy little smoking-room during the voyage from Bombay to Mombassa.

There were no women abroad—a Parsee-owned tramp steamer trading across the Indian Ocean is no place for a woman—and so the five passengers, who refused association with the Dago skipper, had nothing to do but smoke, play cards, and swap yarns. They had told the ninety-and-nine unprintable stories with variations and amendments. The elephant hunter had even essayed the one story which is accepted without comment by the very best people. Now, with but one day more aboard ship before them, they had fallen into those detailed arguments which wile away the hours between meals at sea.

As the men argued the smoke clouds in the tiny saloon grew so dense that they talked without seeing each other, their voices coming with strange effect out of the clouds of their own creating.

The argument, concerning platonic friendships, commenced after breakfast on the last day of the voyage and continued over acres of white-capped ocean until Zanzibar was in sight. The theme was as old as the hills, until a chance remark of one of the consumptives brought beasts and reptiles into the discussion. It was

163

when the first speaker tried to prove that love was all a matter of expediency, existed only among the higher order of animals, and was, of necessity, an unmixed blessing, that the elephant hunter chipped in.

"Love is the most beautiful thing in the world," concluded the consumptive. "If you need an example, see how the Hawaiian women accompany their leprous husbands to the living death on Molokai where they too, contract the dread disease which prevents them returning to the outer world."

The elephant hunter laughed bitterly as he waved aside the clouds of smoke with a large hand and fixed his keen grey eyes upon the face of the speaker. The hunter wasn't handsome. He was a man of about fifty years of age, with a hard, disappointed face; the face of a man who has expected much from the world, but has received very little. Leaning across the littered card-table he looked like an eager bird of prey, an effect which was heightened by the scrawny neck thrust forward from the opening of a tattered, low-collared bush blouse, much affected by dwellers in the African wilds. The eyes were typical "hunters' eyes," bright and unwinking, keen with the keenness which comes from much striving to see quickly game concealed in dark undergrowth, half hooded, like a bird's, from long gazing over far-horizoned, sun-washed plains.

"Not at all, my friend," said he. "Love, on the contrary, is more dangerous and a greater breeder of unhappiness than hate in nine cases out of ten. It is doubtful, in fact, if love and hate may not be reckoned as one and the same passion, in varying degrees. A person strives to please so long as there is the hope of a reward, but once the hope is withdrawn or the reward withheld, the wish to please changes to a desire to punish."

"It is easy to see that you have lived much alone among savages, Royds," sneered Harding, the consumptive. "A few years of civilisation would give you a totally different conception of the divine fire."

"Rubbish!" replied Royds. "The love of savages and beasts is much more enduring and infinitely preferable to that of highly civilised peoples. Surely you must see that your own example of the Hawaiian women accompanying their husbands to Molokai proves that, for how many white women would face such a fate? For that matter, if you four men, who are, you tell me, practically incurable, had wives, would you stake your chance of recovery upon their willingness to accompany you into such exile and discomfort as we are all experiencing on this beastly, evil-smelling Parsee boat?"

As he thus adroitly turned the question into personal channels, Royds leaned eagerly across the table, looking more than ever like an expectant old vulture. There was a long silence. More than one of the four were glad of the friendly clouds of tobacco smoke which concealed their features. Royds gave vent to a little sneering laugh as he slapped his hand down on to the table.

"I thought not," he said, "and yet even a miserable crawling thing like a snake will follow its mate to death and the black woman will battle for her own long after the hope of benefiting them has ceased to exist. The black man loves primitively—nastily, according to your Western ideas—and he has a very definite idea of woman's place in the scheme of things, but he treats her with absolute justice, and thus is practically unafflicted by jealousy. The white man, on the other hand, curbs his primitive passions all his life, and so God help the woman whom he brings to the wilds and whom he thinks he has cause to distrust, for such a man is usually an unleashed devil once he is beyond the outposts of empire."

"But, my dear fellow," broke in the ship's doctor, who had entered unobserved during the discussion, "you must see that the civilised system of equality between the sexes is best."

"I see nothing of the sort," replied Royds heatedly. "God made man and woman. He made man first, and He made him to be master. You say the sexes are, or should be, equal; you allow your women-folk to run about all day and half the night with strange men, and then, when someone treats you like the trusting fool you are, you don't kill the man who has betrayed your trust, as any savage would do; oh, no, you take it out of the woman instead, either by dragging her shame, and incidentally your own, through your filthy divorce courts, or by making her life a little private hell at home; added to which you don't trust your wives over-much in spite of all your apparent confidence in them. At the least suspicious circumstance you spring to the worst possible conclusions, and so the woman suffers without having sinned, for you show rather less mercy in such circumstances than the savage whom you affect to despise."

For some minutes after this outburst the men sucked at their pipes in silence. It was evident from the heat with which the hunter had spoken that there was something more personal in his attack upon civilisation than the mere dislike of the wanderer for the narrow confines of convention. The silence hung heavily while they wondered if he would tell them of that something definite in his mind which had brought the bitterness into his voice.

When the hunter spoke again there was a sigh and a shifting of positions that betokened relief.

"Would you care to hear a little story?" he queried. "The narration of something I have seen; it is not without a bearing upon that of which we have just been speaking?"

There was a silence of attention as indicative of the desire to hear as would have been the spoken word. Royds knocked out his pipe, slowly refilled and lighted it.

"I have been in one part or other of Africa for thirty years," he said. "I landed first in Cape Town when I was eighteen years of age and, with the exception of one or two rushes to Canada and Australia when the gold fever gripped me, I've lived within twenty degrees of the Equator ever since.

"In '97 I was with Wilson up in the unexplored land which is now Rhodesia. At that time there were mighty few farms upon the frontier and you would not find a white woman in a month's trekking, unless you struck one of the townships. After Wilson and I had finished our affair I went back into the wilds with a party of hunters. We struck big trouble directly we were clear of the last farms. One man was badly mauled by a lion and died within two days. Then, one day when I was out after sable I heard shots from the direction of the camp and, hurrying back, found my comrades had been butchered and everything portable carried off by the native 'boys,' who had bolted.

"It took me a month to tramp my way back. I was without any provisions, had only the cartridges which were in my belt, and had to rely solely upon my rifle for food. I had been without food or water for two days; I had seen no game, and was rotten with fever, so that altogether, I reckoned that I was about due to 'cash in.'

"Towards evening, when the fever was at its height, I heard a woman's voice singing a familiar English song. I sat down weakly with my back against a mimosa thorn tree and began to laugh. I was pretty well sure that I was suffering from delirium, for what in the name of all that was mad should a white woman be singing for in that God-forsaken spot?

"There was a narrow foot-track leading through dense bush, which I followed, still unwilling to believe the evidence of my senses. I told myself this was certainly a hallucination of delirium. Imagine, then, my surprise when a moment later I emerged into a clearing and saw a decently built shanty under the shadow of the cliffs and, what was still more wonderful, a young white woman sitting in the doorway singing to herself.

"She had caught no sound of my approach, for I was wearing soft veldt-schoon on my feet and, as a hunter, it is naturally my habit to move quietly. At sight of me she stopped in the middle of a note and, with her mouth still open, sprang to her feet. I remember thinking that she was as lovely as an angel of God. Tall and slim, with corn-ripe hair peeping out from beneath the old Stetson hat which shaded her big blue childish eyes. Then I don't remember any more—for I must have fainted—until I awoke in the shade of the verandah, with my head upon her soft breast and her hand forcing water from an old cracked cup between my lips.

"She told me her name was Mary Shipley and that her husband had gone off with all the boys in search of strayed oxen.

"I felt an immediate hatred for this husband of hers who had no better sense than to leave his young wife unprotected in a land swarming with bloodthirsty natives and all sorts of *schelm*—from snakes to lions. I said something of my thoughts, and at the mention of snakes I felt her shudder.

"'Are there any other white people near?' I asked.

"'None,' she answered. 'My husband and I are the only two Europeans between here and Victoria.'

"'So,' I said. And then I told her about myself and the ill-luck which had dogged the expedition and of its tragic end.

"Two days later her husband turned up. I hated him from the first. He was a 'dirty white,' a boastful bully. He treated his wife shamefully, and was a perfect brute to the natives, taking his sjambok to men and women alike and cutting the flesh off them on the slightest provocation, or without any excuse at all save that of his own evil temper.

"One night, when we were sitting on the stoep smoking our pipes, he told me that he had been a stockbroker back in London until two years ago.

"'I came to South Africa,' he said, 'to keep my wife out of mischief; she had too many men friends. She went a bit too far once; I caught them, so I brought her here, where she is out of harm's way. She's mine, body and soul,' he snarled crashing his huge fist down on to the arm of his chair, 'and I'll see that she gets no chance of playing the fool again!' With that he treated me to a look the meaning of which there could be no mistaking. I should have known how to resent it too, but I didn't want a row, for the girl's sake.

"Next evening she met me down by the cattle *boma*.

"'I heard what Jim told you last night,' she said at once. 'Do you believe it?'

"'No, I don't,' I answered bluntly. 'I think your husband is a pig and I'd have handled him there and then, but I thought it best not—for your sake.'

"She gave me a look that meant more than thanks.

"'He tried to divorce me,' she said, 'but the judge dismissed the case as being absolutely unfounded. He brought me out here to work, unchecked, his revenge for an imagined wrong, and he's making me pay; dear Heaven, how he's making me pay for that which I never did!'

"'How do you mean, he's making you pay?' I asked.

"For answer she slipped the loose blouse back from her shoulders and there, upon the whiteness of the flesh, were the cruel scars which could have been made only by the sjambok, the terrible hippopotamus-hide whip.

"I saw red then, and if Jim Shipley had happened along one or other of us would have gone back to the house feet first.

"'He hasn't laid a finger on me since you have been here,' she said, and again her eyes seemed to say more than her lips; in fact, I read in their expression an appeal not to leave her alone with this brute. 'He never loses an opportunity of frightening me,' she continued. 'When the rumour of a MaTchanga rising reached us last year he went away for a week, taking with him all the boys and every single firearm.'

"After that talk by the cattle *boma*, you may well imagine that I found it pretty hard to sit at the same table with Shipley and to chat amicably with him on the stoep at night. Every covert sneer and petty unkindness leveled at his wife set my pulses racing and the blood buzzing in my brain. I hated accepting his hospitality and yet I could not bring myself to clear out and leave that lovely slip of a girl to her fate. And, worse than all, I was beginning to care for her. I was mortally afraid that the secret would blaze out from my eyes every time I looked at her. I knew that, no matter what her suffering might be, she would not leave her husband, for fidelity was a fetish with her. Night after night I debated the advisability of killing Shipley and taking the risk of the mounted police getting me. I would give anything now if I had acted instead of thinking so much.

"One day, when Mary was away gathering the big lilies which grew at the head of the kloof for the table, Shipley stepped into the stoep with a dead snake in his hand; he had killed it near the building. He carried the reptile into the house and then came and sat down in his big chair without saying a word. I went on reading the advertisements in a five-months-old paper.

"Presently Mary came back with her arms full of blossoms which she carried into the house. A few minutes later we heard her bedroom door close and then Shipley got up and sauntered into the building. Almost immediately I caught the sound of a key grating in a lock, then a little 'snick' as the bolt shot home.

"Shipley came out again, and lowered his bulky form into his chair. His eyes kept on snapping and he seemed to be listening. I noticed, too, that he kept his right hand in his jacket pocket. He seemed to be holding something. I felt vaguely apprehensive. There was a sort of hushed expectancy in the atmosphere.

"Suddenly there was a scream and I heard Mary rattling furiously at her door.

"'Quick, quick,' she screamed, 'there's a snake in the room!'

"I leaped to my feet and found myself looking down the black barrel of Shipley's revolver.

"'Sit down,' he growled, 'you've grown over-fond of Mary and so she's getting the lesson I warned her to look out for if she played any more tricks. Not that you need be alarmed,' he added, with a savage laugh, 'she is only seeing that dead snake I have arranged for her benefit.'

"'Oh, help!' screamed Mary, 'it has got me!'

"Then followed a strangling cry which sent my blood cold. In one bound I reached the door, and at the same moment Shipley fired. The bullet struck me in the shoulder and spun me round as he fired again and missed. An instant later my boot-heel crashed against the lock, bursting the door open.

"There lay Mary right in the centre of the room, the dead snake was beside her, but its mate, which had come to find it, was fixed firmly to Mary's neck. She was quite dead.

"I don't know how long I stood gazing at her in stupefied horror, but suddenly I heard the drumming of hoofs outside. Running out, I saw Shipley galloping off through the bushes. He turned in the saddle and fired at me as I ran on to the stoep. There wasn't another horse on the place, or I'd have had him.

"I buried Mary that night and waited a month for her husband to come back, but he did not come, nor have I ever seen him since, but if ever I do meet him, as sure as there is a God above me, I'll kill him."

* * * * * *

There was a long silence after the elephant hunter had finished his story. Presently the doctor spoke from out the tobacco clouds.

"Hell!" he said. "But I'd like to be in at that killing myself."

The inebriate got up and stumbled through the door. There was a loud splash, and an instantaneous shout, "Man overboard!" but the body was never recovered.

When they came to search the baggage of the man who had gone to the sharks which infest the Indian Ocean, they found quite a number of old letters addressed to "J. Shipley."

Coachwhip Publications

CoachwhipBooks.com

ISBN 978-1-930585-28-7

COACHWHIP PUBLICATIONS

ALSO AVAILABLE

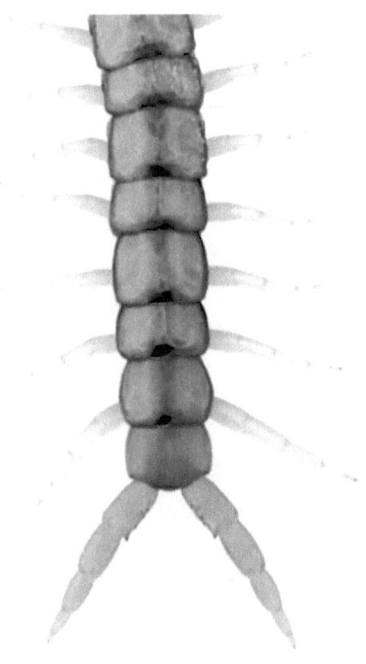

THE GOLDEN CENTIPEDE
LOUISE GERARD

ISBN 978-1-61646-254-3

COACHWHIP PUBLICATIONS

COACHWHIPBOOKS.COM

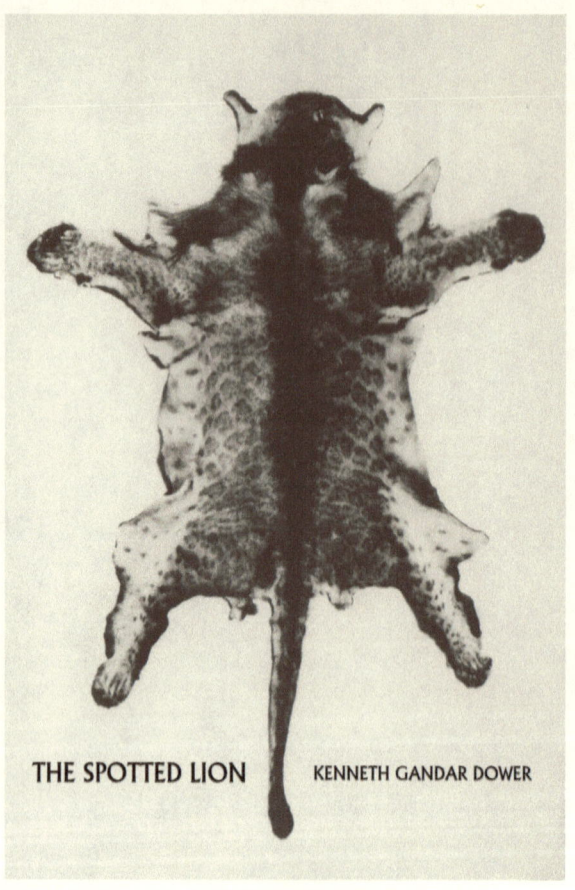

THE SPOTTED LION   KENNETH GANDAR DOWER

ISBN 978-1-61646-071-6

zoologica
fantastica

ISBN 978-1-61646-163-8